Memories of Underdevelopment

A Novel from Cuba

Memories of Underdevelopment

A Novel from Cuba

by

EDMUNDO DESNOES

Translated by
AL SCHALLER

LATIN AMERICAN LITERARY REVIEW PRESS
Series: Discoveries
Pittsburgh, Pennsylvania
2004

The Latin American Literary Review Press publishes Latin American creative writing under the series title *Discoveries*, and critical works under the series title *Explorations*.

NATIONAL
ENDOWMENT
FOR THE ARTS

Acknowledgements
This project is supported in part by grants from
the National Endowment for the Arts in Washington D.C.,
a federal agency, and the
Commonwealth of Pennsylvania Council on the Arts.

PENNSYLVANIA
COUNCIL
ON THE

Library of Congress Catalog-in-Publication Data

Desnoes, Emundo, 1930-
    [Memorias del subdesarrollo. English]
    Memories of Underdevelopment: a novel from Cuba / by
    Edmundo Desnoes; translated by Al Schaller.
        p. cm.—(Discoveries)
    Includes bibliographical references.
    ISBN 1-891270-19-2 (alk. paper)
    I. Schaller, Al. II. Title. III. Series.
PQ7390.D45M4613 2004
863' .64—dc22

                                            2004001411

Introduction

AFTER FORTY YEARS

When this novel first appeared during the decade of the sixties, back in the twentieth century, the world around us was quite different. Che Guevara was still alive and dreaming of a Latin American revolution. *Cien años de soledad* was about to be published. A new man was being hatched and a new dawn seemed to be brightening the horizon. And I was actively involved in the cultural life of the island of Cuba. A true believer often assaulted by existential doubt.

The decade of the sixties was threatening us with the sterile—and above all, boring—fantasy of socialist realism, and was dazzling us with the overwhelming verbosity of magical realism. It was a world in which there was no room for ambiguity and doubt.

Both literary schools, I believe, conspired against our Latin American identity and muddled up our future. Socialist realism is a boring and sterile dream that distracts us from the genius of our language: the mythological dream of Don Quixote, an impossible dream loaded with delicious delirium and tragic irony; in the struggle between literature and the world which was what Cervantes was engaged in—the world always turns out to be the winner. Makes no difference: our true greatness lies in the size of our social and spiritual endeavors.

Magical realism, more authentically ours than socialist realism, obnubilates our image in the mirror, prevents us from seeing ourselves without make-up, without the enhancement of a too often inflamed prose narrative. It hurls us into the clouds while our feet are mired in the mud. Magical realism is as distracting an answer to the new millennium as the historical answer of European baroque was to the thrust of Protestant capitalism and the utilitarian outcome of science. Magical realism is inadequate to confront the allure of consumer society and the onslaught of economic globalization. We need, instead of the authoritarian and closed demiurge of the baroque imagination, the spiritual transparency of St. John of the Cross, the bony denuding power of the picaresque novel, and the poetic lucidity of Antonio Machado.

When this slim novel first appeared in 1965, the dogmatic Marxists accused it of bourgeois idealism, the enchanted victims of the baroque masquerade simply ignored it from the rarefied heights of thousands of fabulous pages, silenced it with, as they say in Spanish, *mucha bulla y pocas nueces.* A lot of noise and very few nuts.

And I, where was I coming from? *Memories of Underdevelopment* carried in its womb the sperm of *Notes from the Underground,* the slim Dostoievsky volume that helped me embrace my existential doubts, my isolation and my painful underdevelopment. That's where the title comes from. The prose, the direct language, was nourished by my adolescent readings of Pio Baroja, from the pages of *El árbol de la ciencia.* Many may claim to detect the narrative voice of Hemingway behind my staccato sentences. Before Don Pio died, Ernest visited him in a Madrid hospital and brought him a pair of cashmere socks for his agonizing cold feet. My answer is the same answer given by Baroja when Hemingway declared how much he owed him as a writer: "Caramba!"

If any novel casts its shadow over *Memories* it is *The Stranger* by Camus. The character is a stranger of sorts in the revolution. As strangers we all find ourselves in the world; we are all passing through. We all feel banished from Eden. The revolution, for me, was an attempt to end my existence as an outsider. It was not a Marxist, materialistic pursuit, it was a Catholic, a religious quest, a search for paradise lost.

Some, I found, read the novel with pleasure; others refused to accept the ambiguous nature of our experience. The novel was embraced and published abroad; *Memories* was seen as expressing a critical conscience in the midst of a radical revolution. "This painfully, ironically honest novel, or testament, shows that place where the anguished private and political selves intersect, the solitary place of exile." That was what Eliot Fremont-Smith wrote in the New York

Times when my translation of the novel was published in 1967. "Not unfamiliar territory, but it has rarely been portrayed with such cruel, compelling intensity, or with such dedication of mind, heart and art." I was proud of that review but in Cuba I had to pretend Imperial Rome had got it all wrong. I was thrilled but I had to insist my book was about a bourgeois conscience, tortured and impotent because, unlike the author, the narrator refused to engage in the revolution. The first responsibility of a writer is to survive, and I survived by claiming that what I knew was my strength was actually my weakness.

Maybe there are two ways of reading the novel. And maybe more. The novel is of an enormous and deliberate ambiguity. That is why today I can read it without wanting to change a single word. And that is why, if I may say so, restless young men and women in Cuba identify with my narrative voice.

The revolution is a suffocating embrace, nonetheless a warm embrace. It is also a dangerous place to write with bifocal lenses. Danger, the possibility that I could be denounced, even arrested, was thrilling. Sometimes I wonder if to write taking risks, challenging the platitudes of ideological certainties, is not more rewarding than to be considered a court jester, a buffoon.

This new edition of *Memories* is the first complete edition of the novel in English. When it was originally published they asked me to change the title. *Memories of Underdevelopment*, the editors insisted, sounded more like a book dealing in economics: so I called it *Inconsolable Memories*. I could live with that title, but I felt mutilated when the three short stories, written by the narrator, were excluded. They said it was just not done. A novel is a novel, and short stories are short stories. Now I can finally see it appear in its integrity thanks to this new translation by Al Schaller. Now it is a novel deepened by three short stories. "Yodor" doesn't displease me: it is, I believe, a tragi-comic metaphor for the Cuban revolution.

Forty years have gone by and the sand castles have crumbled, the heads in the clouds have come crashing down to earth. The cohesive power of the wet sand has dried out and the building has collapsed. The fanatics have been unable to confront failure and feel forced to repress. The dream has evaporated.

Memories did not build a castle in the sand but instead it scooped out a well, opened a small hole in the seashore to retain and analyze the residue of the powerful tide, the burial ground of the waves. Today, it seems to me, holes are more important than dizzying heights; our critical conscience, our doubts, are much more necessary and productive than sublime heights. Doubts to help us understand what happened and to help us sustain our dignity amongst the ruins. I find pleasure in contemplating the ruins, in searching the generous greatness of the impossible earthly dream. Ruins of Rome, ruins of the revolution—it all enlightens us about our mortality, and the beauty of mortality.

What really gave new life and brought popularity to my point of view as a narrator was and continues to be the film version of the novel. I never visualized objects and the moving images of men and women while I was pounding my Smith-Corona. I owe Titón (Tomás Gutiérrez Alea, the director of the film) the miracle of a profound visualization of my words. I sincerely believe there has never been a closer and more productive collaboration than the one that existed between us. Today the novel and the film are one. I do not regret, like so many authors regret, the translation of my novel into a movie. Without the film the book would have withered, the meager volume would have turned yellow, would have been smothered by other volumes in the bookcase. Without the novel Titón would not have been able to produce a masterpiece of world cinema and my favorite child probably would have shrunk and wrinkled and disappeared. The truth is that I never thought a film, a product once considered as transitory as a beam of light, could be the guarantee of continuity and endurance for a novel.

The only originality, the value of this novel is its interiority, its intense subjectivity. Our literature, most narrative in the Spanish language, is rich in fertile imagination and grotesque down-to-earth realism, but weak in uncertainty. A lot of Don Quixote and very little Hamlet. I strive for a synthesis. *Memories* is only a damp hole in the sand of an endless beach.

EDMUNDO DESNOES
New York and 2003

P.S. I hope this Introduction will help our readers understand the novel.

Those nations seem barbaric to me
only in the sense that the imprint
of the human spirit has rarely held
sway over them and because they
belong still to the confines of their
primitive simplicity.

—Miguel de Montaigne

In Marxism, bourgeois philosophy
encounters the means of its
destruction: but destruction
envelops the movement itself as
soon as it achieves its end, and
being destruction, destroys it.

—Tran-Duc-Tao

I am not who I am; I am another.

—José Triana

Memories of Underdevelopment

⸺◆⸺

They are gone now, everyone who loved me, tormenting me to the last. I meant at first to hurry away after kissing the old lady goodbye—Laura did not even want to shake my hand—but then I decided to climb to the terrace and stay until the end. The airplane dragged away sluggishly and roared down the runway; then it was lost in the silence of the sky.

My mother's cheek was moist and powdery when the old man embraced me. Her heavy blue coat had fallen to the granite floor, and she spent the rest of her time slapping the dust off nervously. I think Laura was half sorry to leave me. Up north she will have to get a job, yes until some pig decides to marry her and support her like I had supported her. She's still pretty and she's a hot little number. Besides, I think she loved me—in her way. She could not have given me more than she gave. She will remember me, I'm sure, as long as she's struggling to get by. As soon as she solves her problems, and she does not have many, she will forget me. That's the way it is. What Laura wants in life is comfort and a little romance. I was a fool, trying to support her as if she had been born in New York or Paris—and bourgeois, as they say here now—instead of this backward island. I squandered my talent all these years keeping her entertained, taking her to civilized countries, trying to refine her, making a tremendous effort so our relationship would not degrade into a cycle of "my sweet baby" and recriminations. I taught her how to dress and to read French and North American novels...but that was not why I loved her. She is an animal, and

I'm a bit of a prick. A luxuriant little animal.

It feels good to be left alone in my apartment, with no family in Cuba and almost without friends. I refuse to move; I will not go away. Pablo is my only intimate friend still here with me, and he says he is getting his papers together to leave. It feels good because the life I'd been living was an elaborate farce: I neither cared about my wife's elegance, nor loved my parents, nor gave a damn about being the representative of Simmons in Cuba (I was not born to sell and manufacture furniture), and my friends did little more than bore me.

Right now, I don't want to write any more. The truth is I feel washed out, sad with my new liberty-solitude.

＊

I have no desire to do anything. I am sitting here in front of my typewriter, because my head hurts from too much sleeping. I am drugged with dreariness. For years I've been telling myself that if I only had time I would sit down and write a book of stories and keep a diary to find out if I am a truly profound or superficial person. Because we never cease to delude ourselves. And we can only write the life or lie we really are. Right now I feel like taking another turn in bed. I'm done.

＊

How can I explain how I feel today? It's as if I were collapsing from within, as if my solitude were a cancer devouring me. I can see nothing wrong when I look at the skin on my arm or my face in the mirror; it is all happening inside. Words are useless to describe it. I feel so awful, I do not want to speak or write. I've got to get outside today and into the street. Take a walk in Havana; see some motion, other things, other people. Laura? The truth is I do not want anyone.

Even these keys I am tapping have no connection to me, do not understand me, reject me. How awful I feel!

I just finished trimming my toenails. I am convinced now that I'm a shameless egotist. I spent about a half hour shaping my nails, propping up with my hands my deformed little toes. I felt no disgust, although the sight of someone else's feet, even when attached to a beautiful woman, makes me want to throw up. But my own feet don't disgust me. Feet that spend all day buried in a tight pair of shoes and sweating in a smother of socks. And we walk on our feet. To think about feet is to realize how closely we resemble—that we are—an animal. Maybe the arch is attractive. Some women think of it as a spiritual thing. Flat feet have the spirituality of a slug. The most repulsive part of our body is our emaciated little toes. Everyone should lop them off. The trouble is we'd lose our equilibrium. Could we walk without falling, if we chopped our stunted toes from our feet?

It feels good to move around: to exercise my legs, my body, my eyes, memories, all my senses. This is how I finally broke through the loneliness and melancholy that had enveloped me. I spent about three hours wandering around Havana, watching people stroll, converse, catch a bus, shout, smile, drink coffee. I realized that my melancholy was pure stupidity.

Then I began to check out the women. To examine the ones I encountered as I walked. The most extraordinary thing about women in Cuba is they always look you straight in the eyes; they never shrink from making eye contact. This never happens either in Europe or the United States. Over there, everyone is preoccupied with himself. Believe me, I've sought the eyes of women in New York and Paris and gotten nowhere. They look at you like they would a stoplight at a street corner. Maybe the Italians are a little better. But nobody makes eye contact like the Cubans.

I went inside a bookstore at Galiano, beside the America Theater, to see what they had. I saw a long-boned *mulata*, with spindly legs but a precious face. She looked more often at me than the records she was thumbing through. I pretended to be indifferent, although inside I felt my blood beginning to stir. Then she got up and left. I said nothing to her; she said nothing to me. She left me with the desire to continue playing this game, to see what might happen.

I needed a pocket comb. I had broken mine sitting down in the bus. I had the two halves in my pocket next to my handkerchief. I remember, because I kept reaching to comb my hair, and I was ashamed to pull out this butt end of a comb. I went to a number of stores, but they didn't have any. I went to the five and dime, and they were sold out, too. Incredible, the things we're made to go without so we have to live like idiots!

You cannot find soft drinks these days. I never would have believed that the production of soft drinks could be paralyzed by a shortage of cork to make bottle caps. This sorry piece of cork that, as a child, I would take from the caps, so I could flatten them with a hammer, use a nail to open two holes and make a disc with thread for spinning and cutting. One day I almost cut off a finger playing like that. I never thought back then—nor afterwards, to tell the truth— that a country would need so many insignificant things in order to function seamlessly. Now I understand. We live suspended above an abyss. The almost infinite quantity of details that must be controlled so that everything flows naturally is astounding. The worst affliction you could impose would be to demand a list somehow of all the things we must buy from the communist countries, now that the United States neither offers them nor tells you where you can get them. They don't know the kind of mess they have created.

I couldn't find a comb anywhere. But it gave me an excuse to walk all around Havana. I walked thinking I could choose any woman I wanted. I looked at them and felt they knew I was alone and available, that I looked good, appeared intelligent and even had enough money so a relationship would not be sordid. Really, I'm a *Cubanito de mierda*! I was fooling myself; nobody gave me the time of day. The women looked at me like they always have; it was all an idea I made up. I fooled myself like I always do. Nobody could have known I was alone, that my wife had abandoned me, that I was pathetic and sad looking for a woman in the streets.

Since El Encanto burned down, the city has not been the same. Havana today has the look of a city of the interior, Pinar del Rio, Artemisa, or Matanzas. It is no longer the Paris of the Caribbean, as the tourists and hucksters used to say. Now it seems more like a Central American capital, one of those dead, underdeveloped cities like Tegucigalpa or San Salvador or Managua. It is not just because they have destroyed El Encanto and there are not many nice things in the stores, consumer goods of quality. It is also the people; now everyone you see in the street is humble, poorly dressed, buys anything he sees, even though he doesn't need it. Today they have a little money and they spend it on anything; they will spend twenty pesos on a chamber pot, for God's sake, if someone displays it in a window. It's easy to see they have never had anything good. The women all look like maids, and the men like laborers. Not everyone. Almost everyone.

I got home tired, and I went to bed with Eddy's novel. I found it in La Epoca. I will not say anything about it until I have finished reading it.

⊷⟋⟍⊶

I had intended to note the date and time whenever I sat down to write something. I just went downstairs to the living room looking for today's paper. I didn't find it; the maid probably threw it out. Suddenly I realize: putting down the date is foolish; it's not rational. Today for me is the same as any other day that has passed or is to come. *Feeling tomorrow just like I feel today...I hate to see that evening sun go down.*

I removed all the dates. If something should change, we'll see what I do about it. I do not have to sleep at night or go to work in the morning. Time now is arbitrary. How many conventions one accepts without asking whether they are worth the observance!

Yesterday in the end I spent all day at home. Noemí did not come. I had a strange sensation walking through the rooms that the house is turning into a cave. I feel at once protected and abandoned between its walls. It is an echo chamber when the buses and automobiles pass through the streets, especially the airbrakes of the omnibus, whose sound is like a complaint, the protest of the motor. Stupid to think like that. Machines don't complain, not even a little bit. Though I am on the fourth floor, I feel like I'm beneath the earth. Sometimes I think it's the way the apartment is constructed; other times I think it is me. In the living room, since this is a duplex, I feel like I'm inside a well.

Nowadays I fix my breakfast like a robot: coffee, condensed milk, toast. This morning I let loose a belch so loud after drinking my coffee it astounded me, as I lingered staring out the window at the roofs of Vedado and the sea. I am becoming an animal. Since no one else is in the house, I don't hold anything back. I thought of my father farting and belching alone in the doorway on Sundays. I am glad I don't have to go on Sundays anymore to see my parents.

I cannot let myself come to this. Although no one else is at home, I ought to behave like a civilized being. I would have been terribly ashamed if someone had heard my belch of bestial satisfaction. The belch of an old man who has lost control of his own body.

She left almost everything in her drawer, just as if she were still living here with me. I still don't know whether to throw it all out or leave it alone. I am not sure if her things calm or frighten me. I opened the long, narrow drawer of the bureau, and it left me momentarily stunned looking at all that crap, but I did not touch anything. I don't understand why she didn't collect everything before she left, or give it to a friend, or leave it for the maid. Anything but leave her things here, as if she were still at this very moment stretched out on the bed reading *The Ballad of the Sad Café*, the book she left on the nightstand.

I would have thrown it all away. It bothers me to leave a trail behind, footprints, any object that others may use to judge or destroy me. (I would prefer that only the order by which I have kept my affairs remain behind. I understand myself better than anyone, as

Montaigne said). Laura does not see it the same way. I counted eighteen different lipsticks. And I had said that nothing was left in Havana! I had not considered what surely has been left behind.

Some of the lipsticks were almost used up, but there were new ones also. I kept twisting one and untwisting it. I doubt if anything is more obscene than a lipstick. Sure, the names of the colors are exotic: *Black Magic, Café Espresso, Mango Sherbet, Pink Champagne, Aqua Rosa, Pastel Red, Chianti*...colors with shades of difference. The truth is I never paid much attention to the way she changed the color of her lips to conform to the time of day or the color of her dress. It was lost on me. Once in a while I would notice, but generally I was blind to it. Not since I was an adolescent, kissing some cute little skirt or my first girlfriend, Gloria, have I ever enjoyed the taste of lipstick. I think it was the texture and flavor of the lipstick that excited me most. When I got home to my room at night, I could almost get another erection just looking at my handkerchief smeared with red.

She left all the Chinese jewelry that she used to bring home every time she went shopping. She said it was the only thing really new in Havana. I don't think they let her take all her jewelry, either, because I saw she even left one of her pearl necklaces, the only thing, it seems to me, that I had convinced her to wear regularly. I really believe I taught her to appreciate the simplicity of pearls. What bullshit!

I rubbed between my fingers one of the pairs of stockings she left behind and listened with pleasure to the same rustle of the synthetic fibers as when they grazed her legs while walking. Then I grabbed a hairpin and began poking around in my ear, extracting wax at first, then simply scratching myself, until I saw this lunatic staring at me from the mirror of the bureau. He had the blank stare of a mystic or lover.

I have decided I like seeing her things in the drawers, her clothes in the closet, her shoes thrown in a corner. It's almost like still having her. In reality, she was a composition of all the things she kept and wore. The objects that surrounded her and the things she used were as much a part of her as her own body. Objects are less ungrateful than people. She also left some cheap Chanel No.5. Laura was the sum of all these things. With all the things she left me, I can even make love to her again.

The only thing that really annoys me is she left her Roman coin. She had deceived me there: she never liked it. True enough, the first time I showed her the worn, greenish coin, she made a face that I could not distinguish between surprise and disgust. Now I know it was disgust. When I had it mounted in Rome, we went together to pick it up at a jewelry store in the Via Veneto. I put it on her, while she lifted her hair away from her neck. What was it that sanctimonious Italian told me one time? *La sensualitá provocata della donna...una delle prime cause della putrefazione e morte dell'anima.* * Something like that.

It shows the figure of a woman on one side; you can still distinguish the pleats of her tunic. The other side has the profile of an emperor. I never bothered to find out what period it comes from, nor how much it is worth. It cost a ton of liras. I just liked it, and it made me think of the hundreds of people who had used the coin and are dead now; I can almost see some Roman servant buying eels in the market.

This was what bothered me most, to see that she had left the Roman coin behind. I prefer things to people. That's why I do not feel so alone in the house: the armchairs, the books, the bed, the clean sheets, the refrigerator, the bathtub with hot and cold running water, the sugar, the coffee, the rooms and all that is strewn about them—all these things keep me company.

I saw Pablo. He is as petty as that short sentence. I saw Pablo. What torments me the most is I feel disgusted with almost everyone. People seem more stupid every day; and I haven't gotten any smarter. To think that for more than five years we hung out together all the time! Esther, his wife, said little and observed intently; that's why I liked her. The four of us were together constantly: two nights a week we went to the movies; on Friday nights a cabaret; we spent Saturdays and Sundays at the beach. The main thing was not to be bored. I see now, looking back, that I spent my time miserably.

I believe we hung out together, because Pablo liked morbid films like *Rashomon*, *Dirty Snow* and *Suddenly Last Summer*, and because he had an awesome talent for identifying the defects in people. This more than anything. We would spend our weekends at the beach lying on the sand, commenting on the people as they passed. I will never forget what he said one day when Anita Mendoza passed by without greeting him. " Can you imagine? Anita, exquisite dish as she is, crams her cookie full of black beans. I saw her having lunch today on the terrace." Whenever I see a beautiful woman, I cannot keep from looking furtively at her belly and wondering, what has she eaten today?

Although it seemed but a joke, it struck a fatal blow to my romantic vision of love, even carnal love. If instead of black beans— one always imagines them thick and nauseating—it had been roast duck or molded pheasant, salmon, cheese soufflé, I don't know, even apple strudel or raspberry gelatin, anything but black beans, I would not have lost my *weltanschauung*.*

They taste good, a good plate of black beans, but still they aren't civilized. This is true of everything around us: everything is engulfed in underdevelopment. Even Cuban sentiments are underdeveloped: their pleasure and suffering are primitive and direct, they have not been fashioned and complicated by culture. The revolution is the only complex and serious concept ever to have penetrated the minds of the Cuban people. But from here many years will pass before we reach the level of the civilized countries.

For me it is already very late. Rimbaud has less right than I to say: *Il m'est bien évident que j'ai toujours été race inférieure. Je ne puis comprendre la révolte. Ma race ne se souleva jamais que pour piller: tells les loups á la bête qu'ils n'ont pas tuée.**

Enough of that bullshit.

Pablo is leaving. He is an utter fool. I see him perfectly now; every time he opens his mouth something stupid comes out. He makes fun of society people to entertain himself, not to destroy them. This is the one thing I can thank the revolution for: to have dislodged the cretins who bungled everything here. I will not say governed, because they did not have a clue as to what leadership is. They never read a book: I think one time I heard Mestre say he read a very interesting book: *The Revolt of the Masses*; he had read Ortega in paperback, but worst than that, in English; God, that was too much.

The women of Cuba used to dress like hookers. In the villages, at least, this had some charm: women wearing gaudy, tight-fitting clothes; but for the Cuban bourgeoisie, it was pitiful seeing these women covered in jewelry; they looked like mistresses of some Jewish merchant from Delancey Street in New York.

I suddenly remember that charlatan we encountered in Paris, the descendent of an old family, now in decline. His great-grandfather fought in the war of '68. He made fun of the medical profession in France, saying that Cuban medicine was superior, because it had the most advanced iron lung and the highest quality scalpels, made in the United States. He had no appreciation for the accumulated experience and thought in the best French hospitals, even if they did not have the most up-to-date perfumed antiseptics. They are diagnostic geniuses. Laura agreed with him at once: she said that all of Paris was infested with filth and the bathrooms were from the stone age. I looked at Laura with astonishment—I marveled at such superficiality—and I told the doctor that he knew as much about medicine as a chauffeur knows about cars. He washed his hands two times: once before lunch and once afterwards. I am sure he did it only to impress Laura.

I cannot think of the Cuban bourgeoisie without foaming at the mouth. I hate them affectionately. I pity them: for what they might have been and were not, because they were such imbeciles. Look, there was a time when I tried to convince them to get involved politically, to study what was happening in the world; I insisted that we must modernize the country; be done with the grass huts and the Cuban seductiveness; make everyone study mathematics. Nothing. And then I too sank down to their level. Now I am alone.

Pablo is one of them, from the same litter. He believes—he believes that, since it no longer imports long-finned Cadillacs, the government is going to fall. He is such a fool; he says everyone is opposed to the government. Pablo tends to project his sentiments on others, to think he is the measure of all things: if Pablo is discontent, everyone is discontent, because he is the people of Cuba; other people do not exist; they are only a reflection of his moods. After the Bay of Pigs! He spends all his time speaking of the discontent of the people. That the peasants do not want to work. He doesn't know what a modern state is. The diabolical power and resources it has at its disposal: now at least Cuba has a state.

Pablo sees a line of people and smiles. Idiot! He smiles like a saint before the resplendent image of God. He says the only thing Cubans will not put up with is hunger. With all the hunger endured by the Cuban population since the Spaniards came! The gold mines, the Negro encampments, the war of independence, the reconcentration*…the crisis of the thirties; twenty eggs a *peseta* and not a Cuban peasant that had a *peseta*. The hell of it is, I have seen and studied more than is good for me to know, and I have read too many books. That is why I am stuck here.

He is so deluded, he is already thinking about the business he will open up when he returns. After the *yanquis* have killed all the communists and delivered back to all decent Cubans their beloved island. Ah, Pablo! Pablo! I gave you Edmond Wilson's *To The Finland Station* so you might gain at least a notion of the development of social ideas, of socialism from the French to the Russian Revolution. I am sure you had not even opened it when I came to your house. I will be at peace when you leave next month.

Everyone is deluded. The *contras*, because they are convinced they will easily recover their comfortable ignorance; the revolution because it believes it can lift this country from underdevelopment.

I just lit a cigarette. I have been smoking for more than twenty years and I still don't know whether I like tobacco or not. *That's the story of my life.* Yes, I like it after a meal; it clears the palate. At other times the smoke, the burning taste, watching something being consumed is a diversion. I have decided now only to smoke when I feel the desire, and never to light up just because I am bored. Eddy is right on this point. I no longer wish to run from the emptiness I carry inside. I want to feel my solitude and see where I am going, even if it is to the deepest reach of my despair. Sometimes I cannot stand it, and I feel myself sinking into my body! I just crushed the point of my cigarette in the brass ashtray.

There are traps everywhere. Now I have an irritating new vice: to live dependent on Noemí's visits. Three times a week she comes to clean the apartment. For two or three hours she is in the house, and at such times I am another person. I do everything for her, fully intending that she hear and see me. Right now I hear her cleaning downstairs in the living room. I begin to type, so she will not think I am what I am: a vagrant. For the same reason I light a cigarette, sure that she will hear the sound of the lighter and smell the tobacco. One glance can completely change a person's life. And change one's days into a mere affectation, an act one performs for other people. This is what my life has been since everyone went away and left me alone.

I am nervous, because I want Noemí. She just passed me smiling from the doorway. I want to take her hand, but I do not dare. I don't know if she would reject me. It would be irritating; I would have to fire her, not see her anymore, look for another girl to clean the house, take the clothes to the drycleaners and get my quota of provisions. Life is made up of insatiable and trivial anxieties. What would Noemí think if she could read over my shoulder the bullshit I am writing!

I have tried to make her like me. The other day she arrived while I was eating breakfast, and I invited her to have some coffee and cream. She accepted and at once sat down with me at the table. She really frightened me. It could have been for two reasons: hunger or lust. I am still thinking about it. She was born in Matanzas and is a protestant. She has spent over a year cleaning the house, and I had never noticed the almond shape of her eyes; with her eyes wide open her eyelids completely disappear. You cannot see the fleshy edge of her eyelid when she looks straight at you. It's as if her eyes were slit open with the clean cut of a knife. When she told me she was protestant, I asked her—I could not think of anything else—"Why?" "I don't know," she answered, and I didn't want to ask any further; she was not going to think I was making fun of her. I did ask her if she had been baptized in the Yumurí River, and she spent some time explaining the necessary preparation for the ceremony; the white gown that she had to make. While she explained it to me I imagined myself lifting her, submerging her in the water, so I could gaze at her afterwards, her wet dress cleaved to her body. One could lift her easily; she is slightly built. She gives me the impression her bones are filled with air like birds. If she would fix herself up a little—not wear her hair in that awful kiss-curl permanent, and dress better— she would be very attractive. She has the body of a model from *Vogue* or *Harper's Bazaar*. She is thin, but the few pounds she has are in the right places.

Now she is in the bedroom. I am sure she is thinking about me while she makes my bed. I have a desire to go to my room and embrace her without saying a word, simply embrace her and see what happens.

I do not dare.

Noemí. Isn't that a name from the Bible? I should look it up.

And if she does not reject me? It would mean complicating my life with a woman yet again. At once she would begin to ask me for things, she would come to live with me and would make my life miserable. I am not looking for problems. I am better off as I am. Possessing Noemí would be far easier than detaching myself from her. I always want to convert my women into the image I have of them, and this would take a lot of time. I would be left with little energy to write or think. I cannot allow myself always to fall into the same vices. I would be better off with a whore.

I went to the movie theater to avoid people of flesh and bone and ran into some chittery friends of Laura. They went below and did not see me. I climbed to the balcony, so I would not bump into them even in the dark. Even though I always sit in the fourth or fifth row nearest the screen. I like the images to envelop me. That is why I do not like television: the furniture, my body, everything is larger, more sharply focused than the blurred image on the television screen. I cannot forget myself while watching TV.

I wished to be immersed in the film without annoying distractions, to be senseless to the drivel of my neighbors. It was the second time I saw *Hiroshima, Mon Amour*. I have seen several films already from the "friendly nations"—that's what they've called the "satellite countries" this past couple of years. It's amazing how everything changes, and no one goes berserk! I will not be in a hurry to see any more. They depress me enormously; they smell old, like mothballs from my Aunt Angelina's wardrobe; besides, everything looks so remote and squalid I feel more alone than I really am.

Hiroshima Mon Amour is a bombshell of profundity; I cannot recall seeing anything like it since *Rashomon*, the film that completely changed my notion of reality. Its mixture of love and destruction filled me with calm and sadness. I had to make an effort not to turn away my head when the charred and paralyzed victims of the atom bomb appeared. (I read that even today, more than fifteen years afterwards, Japanese who were only dusted by the radiation from Hiroshima and Nagasaki continue to get sick and die). I have never believed that we are anything more than our corporeal bodies. I believe we are more like a machine than an embodied soul, an electronic machine, but just a machine. This is why seeing such mutilated bodies affected me so. The body is the only thing we have with which we can desire and despise others. Look at the drivel the critics wrote in the papers. Even Eddy wrote something in *Lunes de Revolución* when they screened it.

Emanuelle Riva seems able to accept all of it without feeling outrage. She is green, ripe and eaten with rot all at the same time. She made a statement that penetrated my head like a bullet: *J'ai désiré avoir une inconsolable mémoire.* * I believe civilization consists solely in this: understanding how things are connected and not forgetting anything. For this reason civilization is not possible here: Cubans forget the past too easily, and they live too much in the present.

I went to the movie again, because I could not catch all the dialogue. There were two or three things I did not understand well—even my French is leaving me—and when I tried to read the subtitles, the letters were all torn and decayed. I asked the guy on my right if he could read the letters and he said, "Perfectly." I spent the rest of the movie trying to read the subtitles. I am going blind. Near the end, I asked the guy on my left—it embarrassed me because he was engaged in something else, but I had to be sure. "I see the letters very well," and he stretched his arm again around his girlfriend's waist.

The optometrist says I have a mild case of myopia. I went to have some glasses made so I could see distances. I have to go pick them up the week after next. They say there aren't any frames in Havana, but I found someone discrete, a *negra*, in a shop at San Rafael.

I am getting old. It is awful to watch how the body deteriorates from its years of use; it slithers away between your fingers. So, I have acquired an obsession to exercise. I have a sizable paunch. Besides, it keeps me entertained. Every afternoon I do presses and squats and exercises to build up the stomach muscles. That's so my intestines will not fall out. I looked at myself in the mirror and saw I was starting to look like my father; I have the same kind of potbelly. It was truly repulsive to see I had his sunken shoulders. That was what humiliated me the most. When I sit down, two bulging spare tires settle around my waist.

If I ever might have entertained or fabricated or invented some illusion about the counterrevolution, that time is long gone. They are feeble-minded and undignified, people without spine; the bourgeoisie are a kind of leper at the schoolhouse door, that's it exactly, a disease at the door of the revolution.

Even when they find a weak argument in the revolution, they miss the point; they don't know how to employ it; they just talk shit. The one intelligent thing Pablo said, he transformed into an issue of food. The counter revolutionaries are converted intestines; they are obsessed with food. I think Pablo would like to carry steaks oozing blood from his pockets, as a sign of wealth. "Everything the Americans say about communism is true," he told me, while casually driving his Rambler. The smell of the leather seats, the chrome dashboard with indicator lights full of numbers and needles made me want to throw up. I felt like that every time I went out with Pablo: like throwing up, vomiting everything my family, my job, the mediocrity of the Cuban people had crammed inside my stomach.

"It's true, everything the Voice of America says, what the Americans say, is true. There's no liberty; people are persecuted all the time, the economy doesn't work, there's no food, no nothing. Don't give me that shit; I'm not at all overweight. It's my physical type. Besides, it takes a lot of work to stay healthy like this. You don't know the strings I have to pull just to eat well, just to feed myself. All right, it's true, nobody is going hungry here, you're right. But the thing isn't just to eat; it's to eat well. Eat, anybody can eat. Everybody ate here before the revolution. But the important thing is to eat well, you need protein, you need meat. All those overweight people you see on the street are anemic. That guy, that guy there, walking on the sidewalk, the fat one, that one there, he's anemic. I'll bet you anything he has anemia."

I couldn't stand it any longer; I tried to distract myself by looking down the street through the car window, but it didn't do any good. I told him I had never seen a fat person in a Nazi concentration camp, and he would drive himself mad very quickly if he kept down this path. "I will go nuts if I don't get out of here. No, nobody has arrested me. No one has bothered me so far. I watch out for myself. But it could happen…they can arrest anyone here without having a reason. Sometimes I'm at home, not a care in the world, and I think they're going to come for me and take me away in the middle of the night. I think the worst of this regime. It's the ruin of Cuba."

Pablo is everything I do not want to be. Was I like him once? Possibly. When we drove into the gas station to get a fill up, I was relieved. I have always liked the smell of gasoline; it is cleansing, even a little intoxicating. My nauseous feeling went away. Pablo started to protest because they did not check the air in his tires or clean the windshield. I was elated. Though the revolution may destroy me, it is my revenge on the idiotic Cuban bourgeoisie, on my own foolish life. I swear I was happy when the attendant gave him some bullshit. "Check the oil, please," Pablo asked him. "I don't have any oil...If you want, I'll check it anyway." "What for?" Pablo answered him, and I smiled. The truth is, I am an outcast.

"Did you see that service? You see what I mean? Everything here is fucked up. Not even the workers are for the revolution. Not even that hungry ass is for the revolution. What do you say now?"

I didn't answer him; I did not say a word. I was content to watch him suffer. "If I could, I swear by my mother, I would destroy this car right now, once and for all. Why don't I do it? You *are* a fool. It's inventoried. If I wreck it, they won't let me leave. Not a chance, not until I've sent it to a body shop to be repaired. I won't risk their making me stay here for anything in the world. I had a fender scratched, and I took it to be painted. They're not going to mess with my life because of a fender, no way. I won't let them mess with me. I'm going to leave them a cherry automobile, right out of the showroom, like it had just been manufactured in Detroit. They won't ever see in Cuba a new American car again. As much as they like American cars! No Cuban will endure a revolution without American cars. I'm telling you."

Everything he said was contrary to what I believed. Ever since they took away the car and furniture store, I have felt very relaxed. I no longer have to worry about anything. Fill the tank with gasoline, watch and change the oil, find a good place to park. I used to always forget where I parked the car. I even had nightmares about it. What I want to do is get rid of superficial problems. Since the revolution, I have shed a warehouse of trivialities. A car is a tremendous worry. I prefer to let the machine rot rather than kill myself looking for parts in a repair shop, waiting in line, buying in the black market...nothing that complicated is worth doing. It's revolting how preoccupied Pablo and other counterrevolutionaries are with food. I am content with a coffee and cream, a crumb of bread; things fall apart, they break to pieces, let them break. The wreckage is a tranquilizer. I refuse to worry.

"Look, if I wanted, I could take Laura's car and have it repaired, it's in my name after all, though Laura used it, it's there in the garage, it needs a battery and ball bearings for the clutch...why do I want to waste my time looking for these things! I'd rather take a bus or a taxi," I said to humiliate him, fill him with shame for his mean-spiritedness, but to no avail. He didn't even pretend to understand. At once he began complaining because he couldn't find a fuse, he needed a headlight fixed so he could surrender his car when he left.

"Before you could find them anywhere. A quick kick and ten packages of fuses would fall at your feet. What was I supposed to think when they ran out, when nobody could find a box of fuses! Wherever I go, "We're out of them, we're out," and they say it with such pleasure. They may be laborers, but they're not for the revolution. Nobody is for it."

"Are you a child? Then how does it survive?" I said, conscious of defending the revolution without wanting to, against my will, just to fuck with Pablo. "And all the people going to rallies and all the militiamen around here."

"All lies," he told me, and I knew he was crazy; we are all crazy. Each one of us believes what he wants, although the reality of every moment may demonstrate the contrary. So I offered to give him the fuse he needed from Laura's car. We went to look at it. It was without tires mounted on a set of jacks. I had already given the tires to a neighbor. And so I dismantle it piece by piece. "How is it those thieves didn't run off with it when Laura left?" he asked me, without taking his eyes off the car. "I already told you, I put it in my name." When I got in the car, when I opened the door to detach the hood, I caught a scent of Laura's perfume. Not her perfume, her stench. I told Pablo it annoyed me, upset me to see Laura's car. He took not one but both fuses. Now Laura's car doesn't have any lights.

I have reconstructed this whole conversation to fuel my hatred of Pablo, to root him out of me. I realize that Pablo isn't Pablo but myself. I uphold my lucidity, a disagreeable light. I know what is happening to me, but I cannot stop it. Pablo, Laura, all of us.

My body is showing some gratitude. I have only been exercising a week and already I can feel my muscles hardening. My spare tire is smaller. I don't know if this is really true or just my imagination.

I have my eyeglasses now: wearing them gives me conflicted feelings. When I put them on, I feel like I have a wart on my face; I feel like I've been lowered into a fish bowl; like I am wearing a shell. It really sucks. On the other hand, I see more clearly. Before, everything was blurred, quivering at the edges, like an impressionist painting, and now I see with the clarity of an Ingres. I don't know which vision I prefer. How hard it is, always having to make a choice!

She wore a full skirt, a little above the knees, sandals and a very loose blouse with orange dots. I was on my way to The Embers. For several days I had wanted to stuff myself with Italian food, but I couldn't decide to go; I did not want to go to the restaurant alone. I don't enjoy my food, I feel a little like an animal eating without someone to talk to, masticating my food while people around me are conversing at their tables. So when I do go out alone to eat, I always prefer to sit at a counter, like horses do at a drinking trough. But you cannot do that at The Embers.

"Your knees are precious," I told her, and she turned to look at me. When I got to the front of the restaurant, I saw her turn her leg and examine her left knee.

Then she crossed the street and stopped in front of the Free Havana Hotel.

"You're crazy," she told me two or three times as I tried to crack open her shell like an oyster. Finally she said, "I am waiting for someone, a man I have an appointment with for some work at the ICAIC." These words were like finding a pearl. At once I knew—although I didn't believe a word she said— that I could easily convince her to accompany me to dinner. If she was interested in the cinema, I was sure she was dreamy and romantic. I told her simply I did not want to eat alone. "My food doesn't digest well, if I'm not conversing with someone." "You're a lunatic," she told me again, but when I said, "Come on, let's go," she came with me.

Before we entered the restaurant, she turned to ask me what time it was. I thought she was on the verge of running away, so I added about thirty minutes to the time. "He's already late. I'm sure he isn't going to come," and we walked into The Embers together.

She did not want to drink anything; she told me she couldn't because she was being treated for her nerves. I must have looked skeptical, because she showed me her arm. I took it gently by the wrist, and I saw three or four marks around her vein. A dark bruise encircled one of the tiny red punctures. Still, I had the smoothest, most tender part of her arm turned toward me on the tablecloth.

She kept looking at me with her large, honey-colored eyes, and I noticed the plumpness of her cheeks. It was almost imperceptible, but it gave her a child-like air, like someone who still enjoyed playing with dolls. I thought about her parents and all the absurd features of daily life that will break the spell of any romantic situation. A woman only exists during her youth; the child and the elderly have nothing to do with the femininity we seek.

I found a woman again, when I asked her why she wanted to be an actress. "I get tired of always being the same," she said with her lips drawn. "This way I can be other people, without anyone thinking I'm crazy. It appeals to me, being able to unfold my personality." I did not expect that; she surprised me. At once I decided to repeat something I had heard, read in a psychology book.

"But personalities of the theater and screen are like scratched records," I told her. "An actress just repeats from memory thousands of times the same gestures and words." She did not pay me any attention, as if I had said something foolish. She was not interested in my opinions about acting.

When we left, she told me she wanted to walk a little. We started to head in a direction of my choosing. After one block, I took her by the hand and she told me, "Don't think we are going any place in particular." At that moment I could have told her to go to hell. Then I realized she was frightened.

"Do you have a lot of clothes?" I asked her. "No." So I told her that Laura had done the "*ninety miles*." I insisted that I had many things in my apartment that could be useful to her, shoes, dresses. She did not say anything. "Laura is more or less your size."

I showed her the building, and she got real nervous. "You're a married man," she said, and I had to suppress a smile. I said no, I was divorced. "What will the neighbors say?" I calmed her down, explaining I almost never saw anyone in the elevator, that there were only five apartments in the building, one on each floor. She asked me to go first.

I was a little afraid, when she didn't come in right away. I waited, trying to see the apartment as she might see it upon entering. Elena was not wrong; after me another couple had entered the building.

She stood motionless outside the door.

"Take off your shoes, if you like," I told her, and I turned on the radio. I went to the kitchen to make some coffee. When I returned, she had taken off her shoes and jacket. She kissed me first, she was naked beneath her dress, but she did not abandon herself to me completely. I didn't insist, because I could see she was very nervous. She began to repeat, "I'm leaving" every three minutes and to tell me her mother had absolute confidence in her and that is why she let her go out alone. Another phrase she kept repeating was, "if my mother could see me now." I did not want to force the situation, and we went up to look at Laura's shoes and dresses.

Today Elena returned, wearing Laura's dress. I felt like a monstrous pervert. Then I decided it was not important: to give away Laura's clothes was not a sacrilege. She needed them, and seeing her disguised as Laura aroused me.

Elena lives in El Cerro and I am sure her family is poor. A middle class family would not let her run so loose. The petty morality of the bourgeoisie. To speak of proletariat and bourgeoisie is ridiculous; I feel as if I were dehumanizing people, converting them into abstractions, classifying them as if I were a politician. It's the influence of the revolution: I have to guard my thoughts.

To respect Laura's clothes would have been a ridiculous fetish.

The dress was a little tight on her, because Elena is somewhat fuller than Laura, though not by much. I think the dress is French; we bought it in Paris; it has sentimental roses on a white background. Roses, whether painted or real, are disgustingly sentimental. The real ones make me feel stupidly tender.

We floundered about on the sofa and we tore the dress. We got up to look for Laura's sewing box. Elena removed the dress but did not finish fixing the tear until we had violently made love. She told me that if I had insisted the night before, she would have complied.

Then she started to cry. She said she felt guilty, that she should not have gone to bed with me. "You have disgraced me." I began to worry, when it was one o'clock in the morning and she was still crying like a baby. My mouth had gone dry from trying to convince her it was not that important. However, her behavior left its impression on me.

***

Elena just left. After all that happened last night, she returned today around eleven. I had gone back to bed after breakfast; I thought about changing the sheets, but I didn't feel like getting up. I still felt Elena's sweet and pungent scent every time I changed my position.

She came through the door singing softly in a nasal voice: "Before your lips confessed you loved me," and she began to snap her fingers, "I already knew it, I already knew it." I don't understand. I discovered that she didn't even remember how much she had suffered and carried on the night before. She was very happy and offered to fix me lunch and help clean the house. I told her that Noemí would come the following day, and I took the opportunity to ask her not to come tomorrow.

One of the things that disturbs me the most about people is their inability to sustain a feeling, an idea, without its dissipating into smoke. Elena proved herself to be a totally inconsistent personality. She is pure *alteración*, as Ortega would say.* What she felt yesterday has nothing to do with her state of mind today. The two experiences are not related. This is one of the signs of underdevelopment: the inability to make a connection between things, to accumulate experience and evolve. That is why that phrase from *Hiroshima* left such an impression on me: *J'ai desiré avoir une inconsolable mémoire.*

I wished for more from Elena. I thought she would be much more interesting and complex. I always try to live like a European. But I am easily deceived, and I am underdeveloped myself: it's a terrible feeling to know it. It is rare for Cuba to produce a woman who is schooled in refinement and culture. The climate is very mild; it demands little of people. A Cuban exhausts all his talent adapting to the moment, to appearances. People are inconsistent; they conform to very little. They abandon projects half completed, they switch their emotions; they do not follow ideas to their logical conclusions. Cubans cannot suffer for long without breaking into laughter. The sun, the tropics, the irresponsibility…Will Fidel be like this? I don't think so, but…I don't want to fool myself again. At most, I can be a witness. A spectator.

"Do you like the *feeling*?" Elena asked me. I reminded her of last night's tragedy, and she responded: "Who remembers that? Do you believe in the *feeling*?" I could not stand it any longer. I told her that to forget things so quickly was a sign of idiocy. "What you are saying is you do not have the *feeling*." I began to laugh in order to stop my own nonsense. "You have no right to criticize my way of life," she began to sing, elongating the words and pitching her head to the rhythm. I shut her up with a battery of kisses.

Elena can become a habit. I am used to having a woman always by my side. One always strives to repeat the pleasant experiences he has tasted in life; this is the trap. He suffers when he does not have it, and when he has it the fear of losing it is terrifying.

I accompanied Pablo to the airport. I wanted to recall the departure of Laura and my parents, to see if I might feel something. Pablo told me a dozen times: "I hope to see you there soon." What for? I already know the United States; but what might happen here is a mystery to me. Although at times I am frightened, as I watch everything I used to know crumble and decay. Besides, this is my last chance to redeem myself. When they dropped Pablo off at the terminal next to immigration, I took off. I pumped his hand and told him goodbye. He shouted something at me against the glass, but I couldn't hear him. We exchanged absurd gestures. I did not understand him and he did not understand me.

⬛⬛⬛⬛～⬛⬛⬛⬛

The other day I went to the Lam exhibition. Two couples were there, apparently employed by some ministry (they talked about MINCIN or MINREX or MINED, I don't know), and before certain paintings they could not contain their laughter. A stupid tittering. I wanted to shut the women up with the sexual violence of Lam's symbols and to mock the ignorance of the men. Of course, I didn't do it. Later, a group of Russians entered, more men than women, and they discussed each painting: they would move up close, they would stand back, examining every detail. They were square-shouldered, stout, but I decided that the North Americans at the end of the last century probably had the same look as these Russians. Something coarse, like louts. In Europe, a hundred years ago, they laughed at the North Americans, they considered them savages (even the Spanish spoke of the Chicago sausage makers during the Spanish American War), and today they have imposed their way of life on the world.

⬛⬛⬛⬛～⬛⬛⬛⬛

I ran into another group of Russians at the Hemingway house— no, he is dead now—the Hemingway museum. Nothing ever changes. We had not been there five minutes when this foul-smelling plague of a man sweeps into the room, and starts to wave his arms: "*Compañera*, excuse, *pallalsta*. There; one minute, excuse, *fotógrafa*." I looked him over good, half attracted and repelled; he had blond hair and a swollen face like a buttocks, with a little black camera bouncing on a blue plaid shirt. He waved his hands at Elena insistently, like he was stopping something, asking of her the same immobility as the hunting trophies hanging on the walls of the room. He motioned her smiling to a place beneath the immobile head of an antelope with glassy eyes and twisted horns.

While Elena casually shifted one leg slightly forward of the other and spread her hand on the back of a chair upholstered with a rose-colored hunting scene, three other noxious fumes, two men and a woman, stopped behind the photographer, who kept shifting his position with the black camera against his face.

Always the same. The same tourists as ever. The great world power visits one of its colonies; the emissaries. What bullshit! A little more humble, it's true, and they don't physically own property in Cuba, but the attitude is the same. Besides, what they don't extract with dollars, they seize as propaganda. And the saddest thing would be to find out that they're right; that's the way life is. An attitude very much like Hemingway's. All that the backward countries are good for is indulging the instincts, for killing savage animals, for fishing or lying in the sand to catch some sun. For enjoying life. All the Russians were tanned, bronzed. For them, Elena was " *a beautiful Cuban señorita.*"

"That pose is out-of-date," I told her, to make myself part of this game. "Spread your legs with arrogance, like a man, and extend your arms as if you're about to flee from a hunter." "Be quiet," she said, smiling, the little tart was enjoying her role as exotic, underdeveloped beast of prey. The immobile antelope, Elena immobile, and again she smiled. The Soviets, as they call the Russians here nowadays, grinned amiably, candidly, their smiles pitted here and there with gold teeth. "*Espasiva, compañera, espasiva.* Thank you very much. *Krasivinka.* Very beautiful. *Espasiva.*"

"This one is called the giraffe deer, it is a gazelle highly prized in Africa for the beauty of its elegant and twisted antlers," explained the *mulatto* guide with religious tonality. "The long neck is also one of the attributes of its beauty. Hemingway had high regard for this piece; the gazelle is a difficult animal to find; when Hemingway saw it, he hesitated before shooting it; he did not dare to fire because of the effect its extraordinary grace and beauty and elegance produced in him. It was one of his favorite hunting trophies."

I drew apart so as not to continue listening to his repulsive litany. Perhaps Hemingway drank, I thought, so he could forget that he killed those animals, so helpless before a pointed rifle, as I stared at a table filled with empty bottles of whiskey, Spanish wine and cognac; although he used to say he killed them so he would not have to kill himself. Now he too is dead.

We leaned out of an open window between the antelope head and a poster announcing a bullfight. The four Russians walked past the window and sat beneath a ceiba tree, its fat trunk almost as solid as their barrel-shaped bodies, one against the other; the woman with her hands upon her skirt of tiny wildflowers, a purse between her thick fingers; the men arms crossed over their blue and green plaid and white nylon shirts, yellowed, dirty, diaphanous.

How similar they are to Americans! They're desperate to be the Americans of the future; they admire Hemingway more than they do Fidel; mount my own head and hang it on the wall if they don't admire Hemingway more than Fidel. "They're ugly," commented Elena. "Yes, and they will rule the world." "No matter," and Elena began to sing—" 'Shadows nevermore, between your love and mine'…Come on, let's see the rest of the house."

When we walked into a tiny vestibule, Elena took off her shoes to walk on the lion skin that lay spread-eagled on the floor. Immediately I thought of the women who had visited Hemingway in that same house, Ava Gardner, Ingrid Bergman, Marlene Dietrich. Probably, they also threw off their shoes to feel the skin of the dead lion under their feet. Ava Gardner's feet were very large, almost all American women have enormous feet; this bothered me from the time I was a boy, when I used the *"pin-up girls"* for masturbating. This is all we have the power to do, we the underdeveloped people of the world, to masturbate with the photographs of the world's great beauties. I have no doubt that thousands of Bolivians and Venezuelans, Mexicans and Argentinians alone have managed to get off while holding a photo of Marlene Dietrich with her dazzling legs insured for a million dollars, or of Ava Gardner.

It was a staggering blow to find out that Elena shared none of the thoughts that were swimming through my head. She put on her shoes, and rudely cut the air in a semicircle with her index finger and slapped her thigh. "So this is where the Mister Way lived? I don't see anything so great about this house, if you want to know the truth; books, dead animals. A lot of shit. It looks like the house of the Americans at the Preston Plantation."

It was true. It looked like the house of a clever American administrator; they lived exactly like this. I hadn't thought of it before, and Elena discovered it. If she wanted, Elena could cultivate her mind...she has a natural intelligence. What she had uttered was a subtle idea. Yes, this was the furniture typical of a middle class American family from the Midwest, the chairs upholstered with English hunting scenes, a little table for drinks, the magazine rack, even the bullfight posters. "The same furniture, the same American smell." I asked her how Americans smelled and she answered at once, "Oh, God, I don't know. Like nylon, toothpaste, lipstick, deodorant, things like that. Americans have an artificial smell, and the Russians stink."

The thing is she doesn't deliberate. Nothing festers deep in the recesses of her head. When she says something subtle, it comes out spontaneously. I thought she had spent her whole life in Havana. I didn't know she had lived in Oriente province, that she was acquainted with the great American sugar plantations. She hadn't told me anything. "I don't even remember any more. The scandal they laid on us, my cousin and I. Unbelievable." I had to squeeze it out of her; she did not want to talk about it. "I don't even know. The door was open. A screen door just like that one, we used to bring the mistress her clean clothes, the door was always open, and I don't know how it was, but we entered a room where the woman was stretched out on her bed half naked, cutting her nails, her white face full of cream, cold cream...she insulted us." Again I insisted. "I don't know. I didn't understand anything, she began to scream at us in English...I didn't look at her face; I was paralyzed. I could only stare at the black panties she was wearing, with lace trim. Like the ones you gave me of your wife's...Let's not talk about this, I didn't do anything. I don't want to talk about it." I asked her how old she had been. "Ten or twelve. I don't know. It's not important. My father was out of work, eating himself with rage, they fired him from the buses, and they sent me to my aunt. My aunt was a laundry maid. I don't want to talk about this anymore. It oppresses me. It's why I don't like to remember anything. I prefer inventing things…"

Hemingway's home really made an impression on me. One thing and another showed a profound disdain for life. People squander and waste and spend lavishly when they have things in abundance. Everything here was tossed and strewn about: what had been thrown about completely in a conscious disorder had immobilized the house as it had the life of Hemingway. Everything was stiff. It appeared rigid. But the furniture was placed haphazardly; keepsakes of all kinds were strewn upon the table: a nazi swastika snatched from the enemy during the Second World War, from one of its victims, probably a rotted corpse; an oval photograph of himself during his youth, some old spectacles with a delicate iron armature; fishhooks disguised as insects; coins from other countries; papers filled with notes; a ridiculous gold sputnik. All scattered.

What I really noticed was the austere, monastic feel of the house, of his house. The Juan Gris *Guitar Player* was missing from behind the bed; you could see a paler, cleaner rectangle on the wall where it had hung for so many years. I smiled, I was an intruder here, a grave robber; I had read about it in an article somewhere, some book, like I had read that his Smith-Corona was his only psychiatrist; with every step I remembered something; I had seen him here photographed in *Life* magazine: Hemingway in *shorts*, sitting on the bed beneath the cold Juan Gris, and everything surrounded by bouncing cats.

"Eh? Why is this here?" exclaimed Elena, stopping next to a typewriter upon an enormous dictionary on a bookcase. "Where do you want me to put it?" I asked her with irritation. "On the table over there. Yours is always on the table." "Hemingway wrote on his feet," was all I could find to tell her, touched and embarrassed. "Why don't you write standing up, too?" "I don't know; I think he had hemorrhoids." Had I read it somewhere, or did I make it up?

We were silent for a while; then Elena began to tap lightly, one by one, each of the keys of the typewriter. Suddenly the guide entered the room, I thought he would scold Elena severely but no, he began talking in a soft voice, full of respect, eloquence and submission: "Hemingway used to get up every morning early and he would begin to write exactly where you are standing, *señorita*, shirtless and barefoot; he liked to feel the cold floor of Spanish tile beneath his feet or sometimes the smooth skin of the kudu."

"And where did you come from?" asked Elena, wrinkling a brow: her nostrils trembled. "I didn't see you come in." The mulatto, his round face even rounder still, seemed some combination of embarrassed and proud. "Did I frighten you? Excuse me, if I frightened you...I was with the Soviets until now...You didn't see me? I came in through the doorway. I walk very stealthily, 'like a panther,' Hemingway used to tell me. I should tell you one thing, when he was writing, I was the only person he would allow into the house, I would come right in here. He let me in, because I didn't make any noise when I entered, I wore these same tennis shoes..."

He leaned with his shins against the bed, dressed totally in white, his starched pants whiter than the sheets. Then I remembered; his name is René Alcázar, no, Villareal, and Hemingway had found him playing in the streets of San Francisco de Paula...I read this also somewhere. It seems that Hemingway molded him to meet his needs, the well-bred faithful dog of the *gran señor*. The colonizer and his Gungha Din. Hemingway must have been an insufferable man in all respects.

"He worked until one, more or less, then he would have a bath in the swimming pool. He always liked to take a dip after working and before eating lunch. Here on this bookshelf are the different editions of his books in every language of the world. Look, come closer, this is the Russian edition; when Mikoyan was here, he brought him these books and this little souvenir...a sputnik. Hemingway's works are translated in all the languages of the world; they are even published in Japanese. This is a Japanese edition of *A Farewell To Arms*."

I noticed that he also had Mark Twain's complete works, and I recalled he had written in *Green Hills of Africa* that all of North American literature came out of *Huckleberry Finn*, especially the first hundred pages that I had read with stupid attentiveness. Elena looked around the room; she had no interest in what Villareal had to say, much less in Mark Twain or the Japanese translation of *A Farewell To Arms*.

"Look at these shoes!" she exclaimed, holding an enormous moccasin in her hands. "He wore size eleven and a half," gushed our guide at once. For the first time in my life, I seemed to see the

Hemingway of flesh and bone, walking in those shoes, inside the opaque moccasins, stained with dirt and wear. I had never seen him in person, but now I saw him for the first time, large and solid and playful and dead. "He wore size eleven and a half," repeated Villarreal, passing the tips of his fingers against the dusty leather, leaving clean trails behind on the shoe.

"Americans have very large feet. This is the one thing that bothers me about American women; I have always noticed it, even the most beautiful of them," I said to move the conversation along, and Elena exclaimed, "It's beautiful in a man," and she turned to put the shoe back on the floor. "I have a pretty foot, don't you think?" "Your toes look like dwarfs with over-sized heads," I teased her, and Elena entered the bathroom grumbling. "How strange! Look at the books. He even read in the bathroom," and she motioned toward a little bookshelf next to the white porcelain basin.

"Yes, Hemingway had that habit, every day he read a little bit in the bathroom. That? That's a lizard. One of his cats found it in the garden one day, caught it by the neck, sunk its teeth into it and tossed it in the air. Hemingway saw it and tried to save him. The lizard tried to defend himself with his tail, he was brave, but what could he do. Hemingway rescued it and tried to save its life because it had put up such a good fight, but it was no use. He put it here in the bathroom, took care of it, dressed its wounds and tried to feed it, but nothing worked. Within a week it died. Hemingway picked it up and put it in formaldehyde."

The idolatry of the guide by now was starting to rub me the wrong way, his anecdotes always so humane and revelatory. Hemingway sat in that bathroom and took the same shit as everybody else, maybe with more difficulty. "Houdini," I said, grabbing a book. "Look, he has a book about Houdini here. Houdini swallowed and regurgitated swords and files…"

"Hemingway read a lot, anything, especially magazines and periodicals. He read all the magazines he got from the United States…Every day he weighed himself, and he noted his weight here in the door frame. He wrote very tiny numbers; he had a very pretty handwriting. He always tried to keep his weight around 200 pounds, he took very good care of his physical health. He said that to write, he had to keep healthy, that any illness, any physical malady would interfere with his work. He always watched his weight."

"Do you think I should gain some weight or slim down?" Elena asked me. "You are fine just as you are, maybe a tad overweight, but fine as you are. Well...I was noticing yesterday, you have the slightest bulge on your right thigh; if you're not careful, you'll end up with cellulitis. You don't know what it is? Your thighs full of little balls of fat, haven't you noticed how many Cuban women have thighs like quilts, covered with bulges like stuffed furniture and tapestries..." "That's enough," she answered. "I think you want me to shrink to nothing. Everyone else says I'm skinny and you say I'm fat. I'm going to weigh myself now, right here; I think I won't be even 120 pounds." She got on the blue scales with her shoes on and clicked her tongue, got off, removed her shoes and stepped on again, shifting her slender feet on the black rubber while furrowing her brow as she looked at the needle: "Look here, look, 118 pounds. I am a queen. Succulent, like you said."

"Shameless," I told her, while the guide insisted: "Please, don't you want to see the rest of the house...I'd like to show you the rest of the house."

We returned to the drawing room with the stretched skin on the floor, and we saw a Russian smiling with his shoe in the lion's mouth, between the dead, yellow canine teeth. The guide took a heap of photographs from a drawer and placed them on the desk next to the sofa. "These are from the Spanish Civil War. Hemingway was in the Spanish Civil War. These are by Robert Capa." A chorus pressed around the table. I looked for the corpulent Hemingway in some photo but he was not in any of them; I did not see him. His wife had taken them away with her. Irregular uniforms, berets, dust and machine guns that seem like toys today, long rifles and a man running through the countryside with bloodied face, falling, dying, releasing his black rifle with arm extended, his loose-fitting white pants wrinkled and fluttering and the indifferent grass, with munitions or leather pouches and straps around his waist or grenades, as if they were seeds to spread over the countryside, a *campesino* killed while scattering seeds, an Asturian dynamiter.

Elena left the table at once, because she did not understand death or she didn't know what had happened during the civil war in Spain or simply because the Russians without deodorant stank to high heaven. When we went to the dining room, I found her in front of a magazine rack, leafing through an old *Harpers Bazaar*; I leaned over her shoulder and saw Suzy Parker, thin, immutable, in a green bikini, lying in the sand, her hair red and free, her lips parted, and a wave reaching up her back. Elena turned her head slightly to contemplate a sleek blue slip and she saw me: "Look at that. If I had a slip like that, so pretty, I would walk around the streets without a dress. It's more beautiful than the dresses they sell here by the rack." I pressed my thumb hard along her spine, and she straightened up and smiled but continued to leaf through the fashion magazine.

The dining room table was set for no one. Upon the glass surface were plates and forks, glasses and a center arrangement full of undistinguished flowers, purple and white. "This is how they always prepared the table," said the guide; nobody could stop him now. I examined meanwhile a napkin of unbleached linen with an enormous letter "H." "Exactly the same every day." "But nobody eats here anymore," I responded, yet he kept talking. He was like a marionette. "He would eat two fried eggs for breakfast, fried hard, because he didn't like a runny yolk. He liked them fried hard with toast, no butter. He would sit in front of the wall, here. He always sat in front of the Miró painting, a painting of a Catalonian ranch, a painting Hemingway bought in Paris when he was young, for three hundred dollars. He bought it on credit, and today it is worth more than one hundred thousand dollars…" I asked him about the painting; there was nothing on the wall. "Miss Mary took this painting and many others; after Papa died she came and took them; now, of course, she's promised Fidel she would send him identical copies so that everything would be here exactly as it was when Papa was alive. She promised to send exact reproductions, of the same size, so we could put them here."

"But it is not the same," I said under my breath. "The reproductions are not worth anything, and the paintings are worth millions of dollars. It's not the same." I don't know if he heard me, but he didn't answer me. "The bullfight posters, they are original, right?" I shouted, and he answered distractedly. "Yes, those, yes, they are the same." Those, yes, they are the original reproductions. This is all we deserve, copies, we are nothing but a bad imitation of the powerful, civilized countries, a caricature, a cheap reproduction.

We went back through the house, and I had the sensation that everything had been varnished. I saw everything as one sees a museum's jewels behind glass and knows that no woman will ever make them sparkle again. How ridiculous! I have conflicted feelings. I feel both love and hatred towards Hemingway; I admire him and at the same time he makes me feel ashamed. Like my family; I feel the same thing when I think of Fidel, of the revolution. Permanently torn, I am not in accord even with myself.

"Miss Mary ordered the construction of this tower," the guide was telling me as we climbed a rusty spiral staircase, wrestling at first with some branches of a purple and yellow buginvillaea until our eyes met the tall plumage of a royal palm.

Hardwood spears, long African lances, greasy boots covered with a film of wax; heads of savage animals scattered among the chestnut-colored, rhombus-shaped tiles with green branches. All on the floor.

"He only worked here the first day, when Miss Mary gave him the key; it was a gift, a birthday gift. He never came back to work here afterwards; he didn't like it. He always worked below in his room..."

While he described all this domestic froth, I was staring at a worn piece of mangy skin on a lion's head and thinking that Papa Hemingway never gave a damn about Cuba. African hunting boots, North American furniture, photographs from Spain, magazines and books in English, bullfight posters. In the whole house, nothing was Cuban; not a religious icon nor painting. Nothing. Cuba for Hemingway was a place to take refuge, to live peacefully with his wife, to receive friends, write in English, fish in the Gulf Stream.

Through the arches of the palm leaves, far in the distance, blurred, white and yellow, some houses and buildings around Havana Bay and various chimneys, some of them but not all spewing a dirty smoke, gradually erasing the distant houses, the whole landscape.

When we went down to see the swimming pool, empty of water, I was totally confused, yet I still kept listening to the guide because he spoke in a sweet, monotonous voice: "Here is where all his animals are buried." And he bowed his head; the trees around the swimming pool lent shade to the crude little graves of weathered cement. "Here is buried *Black Dog*, his favorite pet; he followed Papa everywhere; he accompanied him when he wrote, curled up on the floor when he drank in the afternoon, his head resting on Papa's shoes, right here in the shade by the swimming pool when he swam; *Black Dog* did not like to swim in the pool, he preferred to wait in the shade."

Elena came up to us, running. I was watching her all the time now, and she stopped in the shade, with two enormous circles of yellow light that filtered between the branches on her left cheek and on her breast. "And that, what is that?" "It is the grave of *Black Dog*." "Who is *Black Dog*?" "A dog." "A dog?" At that moment the spots of light dropped down past her hips to her ankles. "A dog." She stepped away, walking distractedly beneath the sun around the swimming pool. I saw her when she bumped into two Soviets and the three of them begged each other: "Excuse, *compañera*; oh, excuse me! *perdón, compañera.*"

"The soldiers killed *Black Dog*…No, before the revolution. Batista's soldiers came here one night looking for some men, some revolutionaries, looking for guns, and *Black Dog* barked and barked without letting them enter and they killed him with one shot. From that day, Hemingway began to feel uncomfortable in this house and here in Cuba. He needed peace and quiet in order to write."

They have killed you, too, Papa, the Americans and their retinue here are done for –the rest of us, too. All of us ruined.

"Help-elp-elp! Help me-ee-ee!" Elena cried from the bottom of the pool. "Help-elp; get me out of here-ere." I don't know how she fell into the pool or climbed down. I looked at her from the edge, standing beneath me on the inclined floor of the pool, in the deepest part. I had not seen her climb down; I was perplexed. "But what happened? What are you doing there?" "Nothing-othing. I can't get out-edhout." "Have you hurt yourself?" "I don't know-oh. Get me out of here-ere, come on hurry-y, don't just stand there, I'm going to cry-aiy."

I don't want to see her anymore. I am falling in love with Elena, and I do not want it. The same thing will happen as happened with Laura. I am in love to the quivering tips of my toes; I want to cry. I remember in every minute detail what we have done together. Elena obsesses me, and I cannot let it happen. Every time Elena showed up in these pages, recalling the visit to the Hemingway museum, excited me, aroused me sexually. I feel hollow inside when I write "Elena" and I remember her. I am losing myself and it is going to cost me. Even the style of this diary has changed, I notice: it has turned outward, toward the world, toward other people. When I gaze inwardly I feel more secure. She is a temptation I must reject. I have to break off this relationship. I am old, and she is a child. I only want to discard things, have a good time, nothing more. She will betray me, just like Laura did. She has a different world in her head, very distinct from mine. She does not see me.

I have the impression that reality is slipping through my fingers. I walk through the streets and hear things I do not understand. "*A nivel, ponchado, tracatrán, quemado, teronjoso, mazacote, emulación, pillar, parquear la tiñosa...*" I only vaguely understand these expressions. Sometimes they appear in the newspapers. The revolution has created a new vocabulary. Words I do not use; I hear them as if they were expressions from Argentina or Venezuela or Mexico: of my own language but from a foreign land.

If I continue distancing myself from other people, the day will come when I will not understand a thing,

Until now, at least, I had always kept well informed about the events of the world around me. Now it is no longer possible. I used to subscribe to about ten magazines; I would receive catalogues from the publishing houses, and every year I traveled to the United States or Europe. Whenever I read a French novel I would recognize yet again our social and psychological backwardness. Each new product that appeared in the North American stores made me conscious of our scientific, technical and industrial underdevelopment...We were a population, a factory, of consumers. Now I have no point of reference for anything: neither books nor products come here from the capitalist countries. Everything here has changed, and the newspapers only bring us political slogans.

With the furious acceleration of history—a new generation of knowledge is created every ten years—the day will come when everything I know will be out of style (which will suit me fine) and I will still be alive.

⟶ ⟵

"Close your mouth," I asked Elena yesterday any number of times. When she leaves her mouth half-open, imitating the sensuality of a Marilyn Monroe, she looks like an idiot. She does it all the time when she looks at me in silence. She makes me feel unreal, like an actor in a stage play.

⟶ ⟵

I finished reading Eddy's novel. It is simple-minded beyond belief. To write like he does after psychoanalysis and concentration camps and the atomic bomb is really pathetic. He must have written from sheer opportunism. The argument is infantile: an uprooted Cuban (with existentialist pretensions), after a failed relationship with his maid and another with a rich North American woman, decides to integrate himself with Cuban life. Impossible to be integrated; the man is rootless, and always will be.

The novel is full of stock characters: the *mulata*, the soldier of the dictatorship, the Yoruba priest, the son of the plantation owner— and quaint situations. Everything is primitive and elementary. It is

clear he has tried to please the mediocre reader. But all these characters of the popular theater must be destroyed: they are caricatures
typical of a sub-human world. While such people exist in Cuba, they
have no psychological depth and cannot bring serious literature to
life. They are simple marionettes, cardboard cutouts.

At the end—get this—the existentialist intellectual seems decided on running off to the Sierra Maestra. Eddy wants people to
read the novel and exclaim: "Yes, that's exactly how things were
before in Cuba." To say what people already know does not require a
novel. What a novel ought to do is show people *the things man is
capable of feeling and doing*. Obviously, he is looking for official
approval. The artist, the true artist (and you know it, Eddy) always is
the enemy of the State. In this, communism also aspires.

Eddy is one of the people who will speak at the library about
the contemporary novel. I read it in the newspaper; I think it happens
Tuesday. I intend to go; I want to see what he has to say. What can
one say about the novel that hasn't already been said? And said better than Eddy could ever express with his inconsequential life.
Carpentier is another one who is scheduled to speak. As a chronicler
of American savagery, he isn't bad; he has succeeded in extracting
from underdevelopment the topography and absurd history of the
New World. But this doesn't interest me. I am tired of being a West
Indian! I want nothing to do with "magic realism." I am not interested in the forest, or the effect of the French Revolution on the
Antilles. They will also unleash two or three other scribblers from
the same mold as Eddy.

The telephone just stopped ringing. I let it ring; I counted eighteen times. It must have been Elena. My heart flutters "like a fried
potato," as the girl from across the street used to scream whenever
she saw me. Thirty years ago. "Twenty years is but a dream and fe-
vered is the eye that seeks and calls your name, to live…" One's head
is stuffed full of such crap. I cannot control my thoughts; I am afraid
she will come knocking at the door. I do not want to see her. If she
comes, it will be later. I like Elena; she is not like the idiotic teenag-
ers of my youth (can I already be so old?); but I do not want to com-
plicate my life.

More than likely, she called from the grocery at the corner. It's possible. And she might be climbing up the stairs now. I better be quiet. I will not write anymore.

⸎

I don't know what to make of it. It was a complete farce. He looked like a judge seated at the bench. I don't think he even saw me from that height. When he returned, I think it was back in 1960, he tried to see me many times, but I didn't want to see him. The day he telephoned, I told him myself I was not at home. He wrote an article condemning the New York magazine, *Visión*, the one where he had been working the last four years. If it was so bad, he should not have been working there in the first place! He resigned when the magazine began its attacks against the revolution. That's what he said. Such lying bullshit! He came back because he was nobody in New York: and he could glitter in our backwardness. Twice we bumped into each other in the bookstores of Old Havana and I did not respond to his greeting.

The bench had an old, gilt coat-of-arms of the Republic. I don't think he saw me from his Olympic height. He took out a cigar from the pocket of his jacket—I am sure he bought the suit in the snare of imperialism, it was a blue Prince of Wales—and he lit it as if he were a veteran smoker...I remember clearly. Some years ago we had a discussion at La Terraza. He told me that smoking was an act of cowardice; that people smoked to flee from solitude, to pass the time of day and escape the emptiness that was eating them up. At that time, I smoked two packs of Pall Mall per day. The man is shameless! He rotated the cigar in his mouth importantly while Carpentier spoke. This was the only writer who did not need to dress himself in the revolution to look distinguished. I am sure Eddy felt very important seated at the bench above the rest of us.

Once long ago I had respected him, because he did everything I was afraid to do. He was a bohemian; he lived in an old abandoned house that Lam had left him. He did not work, he only wrote and painted, while I spent my days in the office earning money so I could live tastefully. Eddy accused me of faint-heartedness, because I did not leave the business world to begin writing. At that time, he was something of an anarchist: he used to say that everything was bullshit. Who knew you back then, Eddy, and who regards you now, Edmundo Desnoes!

I imagined for a moment that I was sitting there high on the stage. To a certain extent it would be fun. Everybody wants to be heard after a fashion. Perhaps this is why I write so much now that I am alone. But it is a dangerous trap. If I could live as Lao Tsu recommends: "the wise man fulfills his duties and withdraws; he walks through the world like a man crossing a frozen lake in winter." The *wei wu wei* of Lao Tsu is the answer: "to act without acting." Without attachment. But it is difficult to be and not to be at the same time. To do things without shackling oneself to the future. I prefer to be insignificant. I am afraid of taking pleasure in appearances like Eddy has, for then I would be lost. I am too spineless; I blow with the wind. If it had not been for the revolution, I would still be selling furniture and married to Laura.

We were together under the same roof, he high on the stage and I below among the audience, but there was an abyss between us. The people who have important jobs and responsibilities and appear in the newspapers every day have nothing to do with me. "Napoleon did not speak with fools like me;" I always have admired that exclamation by Stendhal.

No serious writer would speak at a conference with a cigar in his hand. I cannot imagine any of the writers he mentioned—Kafka, Joyce, Proust— having a conference in the National Library. Not even Hemingway, who was nothing but a hack.

He ought to have kept faith with his ideas. To have stayed what he was when I knew him. People get older and they spoil. I never believed he was an opportunist. I do not believe it possible, and yet I saw him yesterday seated on stage smoking a cigar and pontificating about literature.

I am in a socialist society a dead man among the living.

I intend to send him my unedited stories. I have to do something while I am alive. I have been re-reading them. *Believe It Or Not* is how I used to see things once, but I do not like it. All literary problems, said Henry James, are problems of execution. I wrote it in 1953. I did not have time or craft, I did not live in an atmosphere of sufficient literary weight. I will attempt to rewrite it without changing it much. This is how I amuse myself.

He will remember me when he reads it. Eddy was the one who introduced me to old man Pereira, when he was not yet a writer but a newspaperman. I did not treat him badly.

The stories only suggest what I might have done had I dedicated myself systematically to literature. I am going to revise them carefully. I will send them to him however they turn out.

This morning I woke up listening to music. I set the radio alarm for eight o'clock; I intended to go to the Urban Reform to collect my monthly check. Little by little I abandoned sleep, drugged by a wearisome semi-classical music (*music to dream by,* as the records say), stretching my legs slowly, feeling at once both pleasure and pain in my dormant muscles. At other times, when the radio is announcing the news or ranting about politics, I wake up at once; I sit up in bed like a shot and see my uncombed and barefoot self in the mirror of the bureau. My hair flattened against my temples, my eyes bleary.

When I read in Montaigne that his father hired a musician to wake him up each morning by playing some pleasant melody, I felt a tremor of longing. I always suffer my worst attacks of anguish upon awakening each day.

The idea of opening my eyes to a musician scratching the cords of a violin doesn't agree with me either. It belongs to another era. The presence of a stranger would heighten my sense of guilt; the musician would look at me lying in bed as if I were a parasite or a slave master.

The truth is I am thinking in the past. Before the revolution, any eccentric with money could hire a musician to wake him up in the morning, but not anymore. I haven't yet grown used to my submersion in the revolution; I still do not accept that everything has changed, even my fantasies. I can no longer be—I am not the same. My possibilities have been reduced to a minimum. I can no longer travel or choose the car I want to buy or the magazine I would like to read. No middle class variety exists for any good, only the socialist chaff identical for everyone. I have no future; the future is planned by the State. The future of the bourgeoisie—I am one, because I live in "the first socialist state in America"—has been reduced to nothing. The only refuge I have is in my head, and the revolution is feeling its way even into this little corner of the world. They have eliminated the liberty of the bourgeoisie in order to plan the future of the workers. I even take a morbid pleasure in knowing that people like myself are being extinguished.

I exist by the generosity of the government; every month I receive four hundred thirty eight pesos from the Urban Reform. They will keep paying me for thirteen years. No, twelve, eleven years; it has been two years already since they appropriated the apartment house. And they said it wouldn't last a month! I won't worry about the future. We could all be blown to pieces before that. The mushroom cloud is smiling at me. What do I know!

Radio and the revolution put a definitive end to everything Montaigne stood for, listening each morning to the sweet strokes of a musician retained next to his bed. If I rented a violinist to wake me up each morning they would shoot me. They would rock me back to sleep against the wall with rifle fire.

I think, I imagine things, and I am setting my own trap.

I shouldn't write anything. I mean it. Even what I just finished writing could implicate me. Jesus! I can't deal with this! But I carry on. I'll wear out one day…

I have little hope of publishing my stories here. Eddy will not even take a look at them. I'll try to send them out of the country, although it's likely they won't even publish them abroad. They won't get published here because I am a maggot, and overseas because I am a third-world bumpkin.

I'm screwed. Anyway, I think I'll keep rewriting them. And if I can I'll write some new stories.

At least I will die at peace: I will have tried to make something of my life. It's my last illusion, the only one I have left, the rationale

I employ to keep my self-respect, to keep on living…although I fear it's just an inflated balloon, another illusion I make up; probably my stories are as backwoods as the peasant rhymes of Cheo Alvarez. Fine. While I write, I'll remain deceived. I have to take a shit.

It was insufferably hot, goddamn, when I left the house this morning. I decided to walk in the direction of the Galiano Bank. It is the only means I have of finding out what's going on around me. I took a circuitous route.

I passed right by the iron grating of Francisco de la Cuesta's old house. We played together from childhood until we left La Salle; after that I don't believe I saw him again more than a couple of times. (Now the house is an embassy, Vietnamese or Korean, I think; I saw two clean-cut Asians leave the building and climb into an Oldsmobile with diplomatic plates). I do not remember exactly what we used to play. He had two rooms just to play in; we would throw ourselves on the tile floor designed with dark green leaves and dead ocher branches. In the garage, I always used to see a black Rolls Royce, old, polished, without tires and mounted on two jacks. Where is Francisco now? Does he remember what we used to play together? I try to recall and I cannot.

La Salle today is a school without priests and full of scholars wearing gray shirts instead of the blue shirts with wide collars that I wore for so many years. I remember the day I told the brother that my name was French like San Juan Bautista de La Salle, and in front of all the other boys (I will never forget it) he said no, and I said yes, and he said no. His arms were crossed. How his cassock stank of dampness and chalk! His arms were crossed, and he did nothing but stand there squeezing the hollow of his upper lip. He always did this, even in the chapel. Fernando was his name. He was Cuban. I insisted that my mother's last name, Malabre, was French; that her family came from Haiti during the revolution…when the Haitian slaves began to burn everything and kill the whites. He did not believe me. I told him of the coffee plantations…nothing. He made me want to scream at him, insult him, knock him unconscious. But I understood I couldn't do it. He was stronger; he was right. The priests were always right when you were at school. I was thirteen. I learned then for the first time with perfect clarity the relationship between justice and power.

After that humiliation, I decided to be first in my class. Until then I had been a mediocre student. I studied like mad and for one month I stood at the top. But I grew bored, and fell boisterously to the bottom. It was more fun. I enjoyed the mix of hate and admiration that the scum of the class provoke. I allied myself with the most screwed up person in class: Alejandro. One day we each made a fan out of gray cardboard from a sketch pad and we painted some naked women on it with a pencil: with long legs and pointed breasts, in profile because it was easier. The priest caught us by surprise. They expelled us from school for a week.

The next year I met Trolo. His father and mother were Hungarian. They lived in a wooden house near 16th Avenue. He studied violin, and his sister piano. Armando made fun of me because I read Salgari's novels, and he gave me the biography of Napoleon by Emil Ludwig. His father had a shop where he made mufflers for cars and buses over by Belascoaín Street. His mother made fantastic desserts: piles and more piles of *mantequilla* and *panetela*, pastries with chocolate and almond crème. I did not care for his sister, she had freckles and she always looked like she was about to disintegrate into dust; she wore starchy dresses and did not play with boys.

In Armando's house I heard ideas expressed in conversation for the first time. It was a profound discovery for a boy who only heard inanities in his own house: "It was unbearably hot today." "Eat your steak, it's good for you." "Business this month, two good deals..." Armando's father was a free-thinker. Every week he gave his son a peso so he could visit a whorehouse. Armando was a year older than I, and he took me to the *barrio* of Colón for my first time. He led me to this repulsively obese woman and advised her to treat me well, that I was a friend of his. He went every week with this woman to save himself fifty cents. She undressed in a flash and threw herself like a pig in the middle of the bed. I sat down naked in a corner and took off my shoes. I did not like anything about this woman. She was lying in the hollow of the mattress, and I rolled over almost falling to her side. She stroked me to no avail. Nothing. I told her I had done it the day before and now had no desire. She did not believe me but I paid her the fifty cents anyway. She insulted me, but she took the money. Armando scolded me.

I knew I could not leave it like this; I thought of the old adage, "If you fall off a horse, mount him again at once," and I told Armando I would look for a whore that I liked. Finally I found a skinny brown-skinned woman with long hair and a smell of soap and cologne that awoke my enthusiasm and I told her I loved her, and I felt her smooth and fragile in my arms. I went the following week to the same house on Crespo Street, but the madam told me the brown-skinned woman was sick. She told me I could choose another of the women. I left shaking my head...I was very sad, but I called on another prostitute that same afternoon. One that refused to take off her brassiere be-cause—she told me—she was still giving milk to her child. Now I understand the woman was a victim, a casualty of life: but back then I felt swindled.

In my last year, Brother León, who looked like a porcupine, spoke to us in great detail about venereal disease: ulcers, twisted and rotting bones, insufferable pain, deformed children...I stopped go-ing to Colón for about a month. Afterwards, I forgot about it.

I had originally intended to wander aimlessly, but unconsciously I ended up searching out the streets of my adolescence. It all started with La Salle: my feet were leading me; the places themselves were indistinct; I only saw my memories.

On the corner of G and 13th Streets was a convent, the French Dominicans. Laura studied there. I remember she would point it out every time we climbed G Street, and I would stare at the virgin in the niche; a blue virgin, I think, trampling a serpent. Now it has a sign on the roof: Lenin, School for the Advancement of Labor.

I was very close to Hanna's house. I walked past the corner where I used to read (leaning there against the damp stone wall, I often waited for her), gazing at a poplar tree and the electric power line. *La ahogada del cielo*:

> Woven butterfly, vesture
> Hanging from the trees
> Drenched in sky, driven
> By wind and rain, alone, alone, withdrawn,

With clothes and hair in shreds,
Resolution corroded by the air.

Hanna's kisses tasted like unscented petals, like moist flesh. She had very light skin and blonde hair, and when I looked into her liquid blue eyes, my legs would go slack. I used to meet her in the afternoon at St. George School, and we would walk together. In summer little beads of sweat would form on her chin.

Her father was a jeweler, a specialist in diamonds. He always wore wool, navy blue, even in August. Her mother was young, younger than her father, efficient; I used to look at her arms alongside her narrow waist and generous hips, and I thought she would be a more attractive woman if her arms were not so short, her elbows so wrinkled and bony.

It is not easy to recall these things, although I am so full of memories I am drowning in them. Everything is mixed together, the honey with the shit, a yearning for life with melancholy, the triumph with my defeat.

Hanna left for New York, and I went running after her. At that time I was in my first year of law school; I left after classes ended; I did not even wait for the exams. My one and only rebellion! I spent the thousand pesos my father gave me when I got my bachelor's degree in science and letters.

I arrived in New York sick; she and her mother took care of me, they admitted me into their apartment…Her mother treated me like I was her son (I never thanked her). She called the doctor; I had a fever and a diarrhea that filled me with shame. For the first and only time, someone shoved a thermometer up my rectum.

Still a convalescent, I moved to a shabby hotel a half block from Hanna. Every morning she came to pick me up at my room. We spent three months together: walking the streets, going to museums, theaters, stores, walking through the parks, and long hours romping naked in my bed. It used to irritate me to walk on the carpet to the bathroom; the wood floor creaked and creaked. I missed the cold floors of Spanish tile every time I got out of bed.

I feel helpless; I feel a knot twisting me up inside. She was my first real love; she broke through my bewildered solitude, and I bound myself to her tenderly and without fear.

We resolved to get married when I returned from Cuba after arranging all my affairs there. We did not believe in the piece of paper, but we decided it would be more convenient, and I always preferred convenience to truth. I would get work in New York; I would be a writer. Hanna, in her romantic delirium, promised to work for me until I became famous. The first thing we would do would be to buy some rattletrap and travel the United States from east to west. I often told her that, unlike most Europeans, I had much to thank Hitler for. Thanks to him, I became acquainted with her: if he had not decided to incinerate the entire Jewish race, we never would have met. Hanna never would have immigrated to Cuba.

I would like to remember everything for the best.

I returned to Havana, and my father had already bought me the furniture store. I did not even object to it with any vehemence. What an idiot! I agreed to plant myself every day behind the store window on San Rafael Street, but I left my father's house. It was my small and pathetic play for independence.

In those days, before meeting Emma, having nothing to do most nights, I wrote my first story, *Jack and the Fare Collector*, already with the *idée fixe* of underdevelopment.

It still is badly written, but if I keep erasing the colorful details I won't have enough left for even a sketch. Besides, it is something that really happened; I was in the bus. When they asked if anyone could speak English, I kept my mouth shut. I did not want to help either the American or the bus driver. I did not want to intervene; I wanted to see how everything would end. I thought it was going to end in a fight and at the police station. I was the only one in the bus who knew what was happening; I understood the Cuban and the American. I enjoyed the confrontation. For the first time in my life, I felt a little bit like God, watching men destroy themselves without helping them, leaving them to their capricious freedom. God, like any creator, has a heart like a stone.

I worked like a maniac for two years. I sold myself on the idea that in a couple of years I could save a little money and not come to New York empty-handed. Eddy left for New York at that time, and he insisted that I go with him, that the store was a trap. I did not pay him any attention.

A few months later, I moved in with Emma, a flaxen-haired woman (she looked remotely like Greta Garbo) who sold records in front of the furniture store. Everything was more convenient this way. Emma was thirty-four years old and had just divorced the "love of her life," an old lawyer about fifteen years her senior. He had driven her crazy with his jealousy. He had tortured her by making her always walk in high heels down the middle of Manzanilla's unpaved streets. When she divorced, she did not return to her family; her father, a gruff Asturian, threw her out of the house because she had decided to break her vows with the "love of her life." She came to Havana. We lived in an apartment around the corner from the store…and so two years passed.

I returned to New York with the excuse of going on business, and instead of looking at the new furniture designs, I looked for Hanna. I had not written her in six months. It was raining when I went to pick her up at her house. She still lived on West End Avenue. She told me we could only have a cup of coffee together, that she was in a big hurry; she had a date. She was going with a real writer, a writer who had already published several articles in journals from dreary universities like Idaho and Texas. I gave her a passion for literature so she could betray me! We drank the coffee; my hands trembled, and when I opened the packets of sugar, the counter was sprinkled with little white grains scattered beneath my elbows. I left her—I did not want to leave her—beneath the marquee of the apartment building. (I wore glasses then; yes, I remember now; I had an astigmatism, very slight, but I used the glasses as a novelty, not like now where I really need them). She was more appealing than ever; a plastic surgeon had corrected the only defect on her face, a hooked nose. I told her, seeing how the streetlights brilliantly reflected the drops of water on my lenses that "they seemed like diamonds." "You haven't changed," she said. I don't know what she meant by that.

From New York I went to Europe; in Germany the ruins and crematoriums of Buchenwald made me feel even more defeated.

Later, now married to Laura, I found myself pleased—yes, pleased—to hear she had divorced. A fellow student with Hanna at St. George told me, with whom she still corresponded; I'm sure they write trifling letters to each other, but it shows an admirable loyalty on Hanna's part. It cheered me to know that she had not been happy either.

I returned from my final visit with Hanna and the atrocities of Germany completely undone. What followed then was my most contemptible period; perhaps the most aggressive and dynamic of my life. I took refuge in my business. Above all, I tried to rise above, erase my failures, to forget my cowardice. I made an effort of will: my business affairs, naturally, prospered. They prospered I believe because (at bottom) I could not have cared less whether I made money or came to ruin. Right now I want to make these things clear, even if I have to cover myself in filth.

This is the period of *Yodor*, perhaps the best story I have ever written, although I scarcely did anything to write it. Maybe that's why. I had bought a tape recorder, and from time to time I recorded conversations without letting people know it. The only thing I did was leave intact Torres' responses and commentaries and delete what I said. It is a bit long like any conversation from daily life, and I probably will eliminate about a third of it when I clean it up.

It happened in my office. On that particular day, Torres brought me the album with the entire story of Yodor. I don't know why; perhaps he suspected I was about to fire him. He wanted, dreamer that he was, to soften me up. It really impressed me about the robot—as a symbol of life in Cuba—but I didn't tell him anything; I was not disposed to take pity on anyone. I had to fire him because he was not getting anything done. My obligation was to turn out the manufacture of furniture. I hired Torres, because I thought he would be a good furniture designer, but he had nothing to offer. I had no choice but to fire him.

This month I went to the bank seated comfortably in a taxi. But worried: I always think they're going to stop paying me. I did not have long to wait. There were only about seven or eight decrepit people in line at the bank. I felt like a social parasite; not exactly; more like a sharp knife that would never be used. Nobody my age was getting paid. Everyone was old and shrunken, their necks blemished with tufts of white hair that surely had not seen a razor that morning, or old and near-blind, their money tied up in filthy handkerchiefs. I think some were there to make a withdrawal. Anyway, I wanted to shrivel up before their eyes like a prune. I didn't see anyone I know; for many months I still used to run into merchants around town, old ones who would always speak to me about business or kids. The last one I saw was Lorenzo, the one with the record store; he said: "Now they tell me I am—look here! I have worked my entire life—that I'm a thief, an exploiter!" He didn't seem to realize what year he was living in, he even asked me about Emma. Where might she be? Has she left, too? Is she an avenging revolutionary, because I, a rich, bourgeois proprietor, abandoned her? She has no reason to remember me—look here! I am so presumptuous. Maybe she remembers me better than Hanna or Laura, despite my having repudiated her (not from poverty, but from age, she was ten years older than me).

I collected my money, and began walking toward the city square. I was so bored I had my photo taken, one of those that yellow with age from one day to the next. Every day my face gets larger, it seems to be growing, but what's happening is I'm just losing my hair.

I grabbed a bus. It was already full when I climbed aboard; I was sweating like mad (the other day I read that we aren't descended from the apes, because apes don't sweat; although horses sweat). My shirt sticking to my back annoyed me, and the people bumping against me all the time. I felt like slime.

For the first time, I missed my car. When they nationalized the store, they kept the car also, because it was registered in the name of the furniture company. The machine isolated me from my fellow man. I remember how pleasant it was to drive home along the *malecón*, the sun transfigured into a glorious twilight, hearing a song on the radio, some ridiculous tango, like *Uno*:

One willingly crawls among thorns
and in his haste to yield his love

one is utterly destroyed, knowing he
has even been stripped of his heart.
The price of an affliction one
bestows for a kiss that doesn't come
or a lover that deceives,
empty now of love and tears,
so much treachery.

I did not want "to have the heart, the heart I gave away." Over the years, I have forgotten the poetry I had once memorized. To quote Neruda's poem, I had to look it up in *Tercera residencia*. But I can belch lines on command from any forgotten song. I can associate any event with a song: a place, a person, a state of mind, an idea. Popular songs are heavy with memories and sensations, tastes and smells.

I am thirty-nine years old and already I'm an old man. I don't feel any wiser, like an oriental philosopher might expect to be, nor more mature. I feel more stupid. More rotten than mature. Like crushed pulp in a cane field. Maybe it has something to do with the tropics. Here everything ripens and decomposes in a day. Nothing lingers like the taste of cod liver. From the age of thirteen, a patron of the whorehouses. At fifteen I thought I was a genius. At twenty-two, the proprietor of an elegant furniture store. My life is like a monstrous, sprawling plant. With enormous leaves and no fruit. I got a letter from Laura. She is a cashier at a cafeteria on 57th Street. She is certain to find "a good match" there, as my mother would say. She says she feels lonely, that though we are through ("although I spend my life in tears, crying so alone, I will not come back to you…") I ought to leave Cuba before "it is too late." She will find someone soon who, if he does not love her, at least will accompany her in her solitude. I kept the letter in a drawer for more than a week before daring to break open the envelope and read it. I did not answer her. Goddamn, it hurts!

It occurred to me to go through the envelopes full of photographs that lie in the bottom drawer of the bureau. I found an album there also that Laura bought at El Encanto to paste in the best of the pictures. Only two pages have photos. The rest are blank. Black pages, empty of memory.

I emptied all the envelopes on the floor and began to look at them, legs spread apart between the bed and door. The first thing that caught my eye was Laura everywhere: feeding the pigeons at piazza San Marco; lying on the beach, her hands behind her head, one leg drawn up, the other stretched out in the sand; another in New York on 5th Avenue with manikins from Bergdorf-Goodman in the window behind her. The most seductive is a color photograph of Laura in front of a cabin by the swimming pool at the Havana Riviera, barefoot, standing on tiptoes, wearing an Italian blouse patterned in shades of pastel and sky blue pants, behind her was the pink slatted door; but the photo has faded; Laura looks like she has been bruised. The face, smile, everything has the reddish-violet hue of rotting flesh. In another picture the two of us are with the Americans from Simmons, who invited us that day to the pool…

I found the picture of me as a child with my mother, my head reclining against her thick bobbed hair and my little shoulder resting on one of her breasts. Mama wore a pearl necklace of only one string and her lips were colored a dark red. I had the same wide mouth stretched across an enormous jaw (Emma told me once it looked like a twat) and a frightened look. My eyes are always frightened, in all the photographs. Even the one where, dressed in sequins like a real Mexican *charro*, smiling, I point a pistol at the camera.

The one they took at the inauguration of the furniture store is a poem. I am dressed completely in white, with a pair of scissors in my hand, about to cut the ribbon; at my side is a priest with lace gown and censer, also about to cast a mist of holy water over the entire store (he even went to the workrooms in back). And then the usual vermin from the choir and the teenage girls parading the latest costume finished just that morning by the poor seamstress from Luyanó. We all drank cider. I look at those photos and I don't recognize myself. It looks like I am riding the crest of a wave, on top of the world, and yet I had never felt so depressed. I could only smile.

There are three photos for which I feel a special affection. One we took while walking down Riverside Drive in New York. Laura was furious when I climbed inside a garbage can, one of those they keep in parks for empty cigarette packs, caramel and ice cream wrappers, and waxed paper cups. I climbed into one of these containers, wearing a suit and tie, and asked Eddy to take my picture with my hand resting on Laura. Finally she acquiesced and let herself be photographed: me in the garbage container, she at my side with my arm over her shoulder and her chin raised in the air like a sulky model.

The other one we took of ourselves with Pablo and Esther at the pestilential Lake Xochimilco; I even put on a *sarape* and I distorted my face in a dreadful grimace, like a sinister bandit. I am the only one in the photograph that looks like a fugitive. It was during a trip we made solely as tourists, one month of absolute bullshit. We even showed up in Acapulco and saw that unlucky native who leaps from the top of the steep cliff and dives into the transparent water!

And last is the one I took the other day at the city square. The street photographer asked me if I wanted it for an I.D., and I told him, yes. It was easier that way. So he put a black oilcloth behind me, a shorn rag, a kind of screen or parchment roll, and he pressed the button. My face is full of shadows, but I'm not squinting as in all the other pictures I've had taken in the sun. My mouth is still wide, stretched tight, although slightly down-turned (you should picture here the withered sex of Villon's *la belle Hëaulmiere*: before *"ce sadinet assis sur grosses fermes cuisses, dedans son petit jardinet;"* and now *"du sadinet, fy!"*), * my eyes are frightened, but lined beneath with deep rings. I think I affect a certain dignity.

I think the tape recorder is done for good; at best, it is severely damaged. I won't bother to repair it. It's so much more relaxing to let everything break down, get lost—and not worry about it—not anchor oneself to objects and people. The tape recorder and Laura both are broken; damaged goods. By playing the tape so much, I think the friction has worn away or something. The voice comes and goes, but in any case I've transcribed the entire conversation. By playing the tape and listening to Laura so much, I have come to see it all as something apart from me, detached. As if I were listening to other people suffer. I listen to myself, and I understand now that Laura is right, I am cruel, mentally cruel. She was not what I wanted her to be, and for this I mentally tortured her. I couldn't change her. Why did I have to try? It was an act of sadistic cruelty to have started the recorder and engaged her in conversation...a discussion that ended up as painful for me as for her. Just as painful. She said she would really leave me, and she did. I am a monster; I am right to have tried to live alone. The more alone I am, the fewer people I can hurt and the fewer lives I can destroy.

I prepared everything carefully, with premeditation and treachery, but it exploded in my face. Laura was reading in bed when I plugged in the recorder; I thought she could hear the motor and the unwinding of the tape:

"What are you doing?"

"Can't you see, I'm reading..."

"No, I meant, what are you reading?"

"Something frivolous, banal and decadent. *The Best of Everything. Lo mejor de todo*, in Spanish, or *Lo mejor del mundo*. I'm a good translator, no?"

"Right, the movie with Louis Jourdan and that famous model. That older woman, who was she? Oh yeah, Joan Crawford, I remember now, about the career women..."

"That's what I want to be, a career woman; I'm tired of being a rich, frivolous, kept woman. We may be married, but I live like a kept woman. I'd like to be a woman efficient in business and passionate in love...you can't live glamorously here, that's why we should live in New York."

"Your skin deserves the best. Do you believe your skin deserves *lo mejor del mundo*?"

"Why not? Let me go on reading...What are you doing just sitting there staring at me? You know I can't read or do anything when you stare at me like that, analyzing me like I was a rare bug..."

"Why don't we talk a while?"

"*What's come over you?* What bug has bitten you?"

"A rare bug. What bug has bitten you? You love to talk so much about bugs all of a sudden…"

"What should I talk about? Cuba is a country full of bugs, filthy people, riff-raff. It's a backward country, according to you…"

"And you, what do you think?"

"Where did that come from? You never care what I think, about anything. Really, *what's come over you?*"

"You're practicing your English a lot . … I think you really want to leave."

"Well, this is too much. It was you, you yourself insisted that I study English…for trips, for reading English novels, and now you criticize me. I don't understand you. I have never understood you."

"Don't be a bitch."

"Why not? I'm a bitch, so what?"

"Keep it up, come on, you know how much I love you like this, when you turn crude, how erotic it makes me feel, when you're torn between elegance and vulgarity, sophistication and smut."

"I've been watching you lately, and each day you act more and more ugly. What is happening to you? You seem, I don't know, you are in the most foul mood lately…"

"It's because I can't find *Yardley* hair oil, or *Colgate* toothpaste, or imperialist after shave lotion; as you know these things help to…"

"This again. We need a vacation."

"You, however, are more attractive every day."

"But I am growing old. Already…"

"It doesn't matter, beauty is something artificial and you are more artificial every day. Me, I don't care for youthful, natural beauty, I like women like you, artificially constructed with education, good food, exercise, nice clothes, makeup . . Thanks to these things, you have left the Cuban riff-raff behind, transformed into an elegant, sparkling woman…"

"You are attacking me, I won't endure it. I never know if you are speaking seriously or making fun…"

"A little of both…"

"Fine, go make fun of your mother…"

"Ha, ha, ha…"

"Up yours…"

"Very good."

"And if you don't want me talking like this you can throw me out of here right now. I can't bear to keep living here….I will not sleep in the same bed with you any more. I won't endure making love without the air conditioner, the thing is still broken; I can't stand it when I start to sweat and you get sticky, you sweat too much, you sweat like an animal…"

"I should tell you something, everything you've said is being taped………"

"No, I can't believe it. You wouldn't do that to me…"

"Well, yes, it's all recorded, every word you have said is on that tape you see turning around there on the recorder. Don't look so hard, there below, on the floor."

"You're a bastard. I'll never forgive you, never; you're a monster, a beast, I'll break that piece of shit…"

"Don't do that, don't do that."

"What do you want, that I start kicking you?"

"It's preferable…"

"I will not give you this pleasure. You and I are through. I don't want to look at you; I don't want to see you ever again. I'll go away alone, I don't want you coming North with me any more. You don't interest me. I will go alone; I will go to the United States alone. I'll not endure another day here."

"Stop kicking the machine…"

"I'll kick it if I feel like it. After I'm gone, you won't be able to play with your toy any more. I'm sure you'll find some other woman to torture like you've tortured me…At least you won't be able to tape the voices of any of your whores, because whores are the only people staying here in Cuba…"

"You're going to leave me here alone."

"I am going to leave you alone and alone and alone…with your tape recorder. On top of that, I am tired of being treated like a laboratory rat for your little whims and games. I have my life to live, I am already getting old; I'll soon be thirty-five. I am going; I am going. I am going alone. I don't need you anymore. You and I are through."

"You are leaving me now, because times are tough. You didn't say you would love me forever."

"I am going, I am going…"

"You didn't say you would wait for me, that we'd go together…"

"I am going alone…"

"So you are leaving me…"

"I am leaving you and I am going alone."

⸻ ⸻

The fellow treated me with tweezers. He spoke to me respectfully: "look, I don't want to bother you," "it's a very delicate matter," "my sister is a respectable girl," "put yourself in my place": but he had a sinister appearance, with his widely pleated pants hanging from his hips like the sails of a ship.

I assumed an appropriate dignity, but I was concerned. I looked at him, and I could not understand why he hadn't come at me with both fists. That was what I feared. My apparent calm had nothing to do with the ideas that whirled through my head.

He told me that Elena was a virgin before she met me and that my obligation was to marry her. The sooner the better. I said yes to him, to get the upper hand. Whenever matters are driven by words and rationality, I have the advantage. I insisted that I had not violated his sister. I asked to speak with Elena, I became sentimental; I told him that first Elena must tell me everything to my face. "You have disgraced her, " the fellow insisted. "You have disgraced her."

All this because for over a week I had not answered the door. Elena had called by telephone; she had pounded on the door: I neither answered the phone nor let her inside. Women are vipers when they feel rejected. I was disposed to deny everything all the way. I wanted her to accuse me, to say everything to my face, so I could deny it outright. Of course, I wanted nothing to do with the police; I was inclined to marry Elena, if she asked me. I would rather her family eat me like a duck a thousand times —I was sure she had an infinite set of relations—than rot in a jail cell.

The little brother wanted to find Elena immediately, but I insisted it would be better that night. He agreed. Not on my account: it was lunch hour and he had to return to work. He said something I didn't understand about "absenteeism."

If I had only heard him we would have parted on friendly terms, but he looked malicious when I cautiously held his gaze.

We arranged to meet at El Carmelo; I told him I ate there every night. I did not want him returning to my apartment. I did not want him looking into my apartment again, inside the cavern of my living room. Besides, El Carmelo was a good place to humble him, it had air-conditioning and a residual bourgeois ambience; it was sure to make him uncomfortable, I thought, and it would cut him down to size.

I was disposed to marry her. It was better than going to jail for corrupting a minor. I felt miserable, cornered; from time to time I felt like rebelling, telling him to go to hell, but fear pacified me.

When I sat down alone to eat at El Carmelo, while I was waiting for them, it occurred to me that I might have made a mistake. If the atmosphere would humiliate them, they would humiliate me with their presence. None of this was important: I was disposed to let them work me over. I was positive, however, that she was no virgin. That crap her mother said about blood on her daughter's panties. Don't get me started.

For the past month I haven't been able to write anything. Just to remember some of the scenes I endured fills me with dread; I feel the steam of sweat, the bad breath and stench of the prisoners. An ambiguous terror, all of it.

Elena insisted that I had "disgraced" her. Imagine, with the sensuality of the tropics, to talk of sex as if it were a disgrace! I was imperturbable. I played the victim: I acquiesced. I would marry Elena. "But you must do it now, at once," shouted her devil of a brother. I told him: "I don't know what papers are needed." (I had not told him I was still married to Laura). Elena said without looking at me that I had deceived her, that I had promised her, that it was the first time, she never; she was blushing. But in spite of their insults, I spilled everything. Even her attack of tears after we first made love. Everyone stared at us from the other tables.

We left to meet with her parents, who were waiting on the cor-

ner. On Línea Street, seated on a bench in front of the parish church.
I remembered that as a boy I often used to sit there with Pablo. How
everything has changed! Which depressed me even more. They wanted
to screw me good, but they are simple-minded.

"My little girl, my beautiful little girl, we raised her like she
was crystal," the mother cried. The father scarcely spoke; from time
to time he would draw near and push me or grab my shirt; that was
all he did. The mother insisted that Elena had returned that night
with "her panties spotted with blood." I was afraid; I felt sorry for
Elena and for her parents and brother; I was depressed, I was afraid
they would throw me in jail. "We took care of her, we pampered her,
her health is so delicate." In less than a minute, the mother played
another record and began to insult me: "Degenerate son of a bitch,
what you have done to my daughter doesn't have a name..." and
then she drew her hand over her face as if she wanted to erase its
features.

The brother, as he had been promising me, called a cop and we
were escorted to the police station. I don't even know which number
it was: somewhere over by Prince Hill...about one step away from
the prison. They drew up a statement, while the mother cried like a
baby and the father grabbed me by the shirt. The brother did everything: he made the formal complaint, he talked a lot of bop; he tried
to marry me off to Elena right there. The loud clatter from the massive typewriter sounded like pistol shots. Each time the carriage arrived at the end of the row the bell of damnation rang out. I said yes
to everything. My tongue was cleaved to my mouth.

They put me in a cell at the station with six or seven other fellows. I was scared. I couldn't look anyone in the face. I didn't know
how to act. "If they insult me what should I do? I cannot cry out. If I
so much as squeak, they'll fix me good." I looked at the walls, peeled
and dirty. One man, hairy and with tiny little eyes sunk deep in his
face, approached and asked me: "Why did they put you here?" I told
the truth; I affected a husky voice and spoke but few words; I offered
him a cigarette. When they saw that it was American, they all fell on
me at once. They cleaned me out. "You aren't Cuban," said one. I
told him, yes, I was Cuban; they didn't believe me. I did not insist: I
told a lie, a stupid one. "My mother is a foreigner, from France, and

my father is Cuban. You're right. I lived outside of Cuba for many years." All lies. I heard myself speak as if I were some other person in the jail cell saying it, and I felt miserable. I invented a whole history so as not to defraud the insight of a thief.

I felt naked, exposed to a way of thinking and acting that was totally foreign to me. My first time in jail. I promised myself not to converse with anybody and always to use simple gestures. I wallowed on the floor, so they would not think I was preoccupied with keeping my clothes clean and wouldn't notice the difference between my New York clothes and the shirts and pants, most likely bought on Monte Street, that surrounded me. If they saw me being too fastidious, I was sure they would get ideas and I would be the one to pay.

There was a deaf mute in the cell. He moaned when he spoke, and nobody could clearly understand the signs that he made. He had a desperate look; he was frantic. They said he had been picked up for fondling a woman in the street. Not for the first time. He was a feeble, skinny fellow. He had the anxious eyes of a dog, a little moist and mute, like his mouth.

I wanted to commit suicide. Never again would I be thrown...I can't talk about this.

Early in the morning they took one fellow away, the tallest one of the group, who had started to sing as dawn was breaking, "lie to me again, let your wickedness be my joy." I think it was the first time in my life I felt envious of someone. I wanted to flee from the cell and station. I was exhausted from having so many people around me, staring at me, dreaming up lies about me. I couldn't relax. Sweat and piss, dampness and shit and bad breath. Everything was sticky and uncomfortable. I was desperate to be left alone, alone. I thought that just to leave here and walk down the street—like that tall fellow was sure to do—would be the greatest happiness. To walk through the streets free, to breathe deeply and to look at people and move among them seemed to me all the happiness to which a man could aspire.

Later they took away all my companions and left me alone in the cell. All of them went to the penitentiary at Prince Hill. To the rock pile. A little later they would take me to court. I felt fine by myself. The floor was dirty, the walls were wet and peeling, there was nothing comfortable in the entire cell, and yet I felt fine. People are what drive me to despair. I cannot endure spending much time close to anyone. Nothing is more loathsome than lots of people crammed together. That's why so many of us, enclosed inside our houses, dream of walking alone on a deserted beach. A man alone is a considerable being, and many men together are a disgrace.

I could live in a cell with delight like the Count of Monte Cristo. Anybody could. What's so awful is having to share the same existence with hundreds of prisoners, stares and desires. Someone else's stares and desires. This defines the modern age: even in a jail cell, you cannot escape the masses.

I decided not to marry Elena. I don't know where I found the strength to resist the trap that was being set for me. Nor do I believe in doing something out of pity. Suddenly I preferred the jail cell to a life of deceit. I did not want to marry Elena, and I was prepared to face the consequences. They had me cornered too securely: you cannot do that to a man. Though the mother may die of shame and the father grip my shirt until his arms fall off. Though the brother may rain me with punches. I simply was not prepared to fall into another trap. I was sitting in a jail cell, feeling like a piece of shit, and I did not want to marry Elena. I decided this while I was alone in the cell. If I had still been crammed in with the other prisoners, I would have gotten married just to escape the presence of so many strange companions.

They escorted me to the High Court, behind the confectionery tower of the Plaza of the Revolution and the statue of Martí.

I said the girl was not a virgin.

The mother continued to cry; the brother and father could not explain their case. I was on the verge of tears. They referred to me as the "deceased;" I am sure they had seen the word in some police report. They tangled themselves up trying to employ legal terminology. The brother said I had "profaned his sister in abundance." I was the only one who spoke with any coherence. I don't know how, but I explained everything with clarity. That was my undoing. At once, the judge began to treat me as if I had used my diabolical skill and intelligence to deceive an unfortunate innocent—"the people;" everything now is "the people." He treated me like I was a common criminal.

I realized that Cuba had been turned upside down. Or right side up, it's possible. Everything had changed. Before, I would have been the respectable innocent and they the guilty unfortunates. Now, I was the one to suffer. They, with their poverty, their incoherence, and the prejudices that once had stigmatized them, were all respectable people. I was guilty by my education.

I asked that they give Elena a physical examination. That they examine her to determine whether I had violated her.

Then they unveiled Elena's madness. The mother insisted Elena was insane. That was her word, insane. This completed my transformation into a soulless monster. I had always known that Elena was a bit abnormal. But who isn't abnormal in this day and age!

I recalled what she said in the restaurant about her double personality.

Her mother said they were a "decent" family, that "my poor daughter is sick…I take care of her…this man is a degenerate, a monster, a criminal…"

I declared that I had no idea the girl was deranged, that I had met her in the street, that her mental illness was not apparent at first glance, that at the time she had full use of her mental faculties, that one could not see any illness at first sight…the judge ordered me to be silent.

Just before the medical examination, it came to light that Elena had been a literacy tutor and afterwards was awarded a government scholarship. Now I was totally undone. I held my breath. The judge took notes.

The verdict:

"Whereas: the plaintiffs in the present suit allege that the accused, whose personal information and domicile are on the record by writ, had led a minor of sixteen years of age, named Elena Josefa Dorado, by deception to his apartment, in which place he possessed the virginity of the same, in spite of finding the same disturbed in her mental faculties."

"Whereas: upon examination by the forensic doctors of this court, they reported: that they have examined Elena Josefa on the premises of this court, who by her physical appearance, hair samples and dental history show her to have completed between sixteen and

seventeen years of age. Extensive examination of her external geni-
tal organs shows the complete rupture of the hymen, of no recent
date. Investigation of her mental state shows, by examination and
practical interrogation of the same, that she enjoys her full mental
faculties."

"Whereas: upon examination of her prior record it was discovered that on August 23rd past, Elena Josefa was detained in the lobby
of the Free Havana Hotel on suspicion of engaging in prostitution
with foreign visitors, for which her temporary internment is recom-
mended in a place adequate for her treatment and rehabilitation by
medical specialists."

"Now therefore: because these facts do not possess the charac-
teristics of the crime of rape, defined and punishable by article 482-
A-B-2 of the Code of Social Defense and by common law, no proof
of criminality exists to conduct a prosecution against the accused."

"By article 384 ff. of the Application of the Law of Criminal
Sentencing and Order 109 of 1889, this court declares that the accused is tried and subject to the findings of the present case, and his
immediate release is decreed."

I have not seen Elena again, nor her brother, nor her father and
mother. I hope they have not shut her away. I am the guilty one; they
are right. There is something, an ethic, something, that leaves me
very badly stained. I have seen too much to be innocent. Their minds
are too shrouded in darkness to be guilty.

I have always been of two minds when it comes to women: they
have given me my greatest pleasures, and they've occasioned the
worst ordeals of my life. I only feel truly at ease with a book, seeing
a painting, watching a movie; but all that's an illusion. A woman is a
book, a movie, a painting, but she is real.

The hell of it is: man has a dual nature, he can't do anything
good without tripping himself up, and he can't do anything bad
without helping someone. Everything good also causes pain,

and everything bad profits us at the same time. Something like that.

I went to bed after lunch and right away my book slipped out of my hands. I woke up suddenly like I had rolled off a cliff. I couldn't grab hold of anything; the objects in my house, stiff and cold, had no connection to me.

It only lasted a few minutes, but it had been the most violent anguish attack...no, not anguish attack; but the most profound rupture I've ever felt between my conscious being and the outside world. I cannot explain it adequately; words betray me, turning it all flat and insignificant.

Deeply embedded in one's consciousness is the dread of obliteration and loss of identity, the security of knowing "my name is such and such," the fear of losing one's connection to the pleasure and even the pain of everything we have and know...I long to know whether something exists beyond this abyss, this abandonment and chaos that engulfs me. If something more real exists once the mind has ceased to cram us with ideas, desires and emotions. It is a silence that appears inherently as terror, terror before that emptiness-silence-space, that I could not accept.

Every time my mother writes me from up North she puts inside the letter a stick of gum and a pack of blue Gillette razor blades. She knows I don't chew gum, and I shave with an electric razor. I can barely understand the old man's writing. They're lunatics. I don't tell them anything, because I always answer the letters with a post card. That way I don't have to invent any news. I tell them I am fine and all.

The only thing I've asked them to send me is magazines and books, but I get nothing. They wrap and send me cans of ham, and cereals, and Nescafé and cartons of cigarettes. A disaster. We do not begin to understand each other.

I've irritated the tip of my tongue from poking at a cavity I just found in a molar. Every now and again it emits a horrible stab of pain. I am going to the dentist this afternoon. I'll go, because I am more afraid of losing the tooth than I am of the "machine."

I feel better, although besides this one cavity he discovered three more. No problem. I jumped the first hurdle, and the hardest thing to do in the world is start something…and to know when to stop. In this case it all depends on the dentist. I go back on Friday. From the moment I sat down in the chair, I began to moan—"ah, ah, ah"—just from thinking he would touch a nerve with the burr. It is a kind of ball full of spikes attached to a shaft, like they used in hand-to-hand combat in the Middle Ages, the difference being that men in those days would flee from the blow, and today they submit to the torture of the dentist voluntarily.

Fear is always the same. I was watching myself. My fear arose, because I didn't want to accept the reality of the dentist, I wanted to run away; once I accepted its inevitability I felt peaceful, composed. We suffer, because we don't want to suffer. If I could overcome my fear of people and death with the same ease that I dissolved my fear of the drill, I would be another man!

Tomorrow I'll go to the pool at the Havana Riviera for a swim; I think they rent the cabins now to anyone. I will catch a little sun; see if it will massage my brain.

It is two in the morning and I cannot sleep. I don't dare even to lean my back against the chair; I move my shoulders a little, and it feels like I've been pricked by a million needles. My skin is burning. This and it rained in the afternoon.

While I took in a little sun, I attended on the people around me. Most of them are exhibitionists. The athletic types parade around with all the finesse of a cinematic monster. First they make their entrance, walking slowly, their gait something between the elegance of a panther and the swagger of a gorilla. They laugh, greet effusively three or four people scattered around the pool...A truly magical moment occurs when they are about to have a swim. They stop at the very edge of the pool, their muscles tensed, and when you think they are going to dive in, they take a step back...they repeat this three or four times. The spell is broken when they finally dive in headfirst: once they're in the water. The moment that attracts the most attention is the precise instant before they launch themselves into the water; they know it, instinctively, because I don't think they can rationalize their actions. In horror films also, the most electrifying moment is the instant just before the appearance of the monster or assassin.

Sometimes they do some shadow boxing. I can't tell if this is to impress the ladies or because they just want to mess with each other.

A gnarled pit of a woman strutted around as if she were a savory plum. Everybody thinks they have something to offer. Maybe she had a pretty heel. I didn't manage to see her up close.

Everything is pure spectacle when one does not participate in the game. That's why I would rather read.

I began to observe the different ages of the women. There is one exquisite moment, between thirty and thirty-five years, when Cuban women pass suddenly from ripeness to decay. They are like fruit that decompose with astonishing speed. With the same giddy speed as the afternoon sun sinking into the sea.

It's an intoxicating game to scrutinize just a single part of a person's body. The ears, for example, or the abdomen. Not to mention the shapes, positions, and sizes of a woman's hips. The "s" that shapes the waist and buttocks of the Cuban woman sometimes wriggles free of the rest of her body, acquires a personality of its own.

In general, the people impressed me as hapless, defenseless, nearly hairless animals precariously balanced on two feet...Like the surrealists, I believe the intelligence and physical imperfection of man is due to his origination from the premature fetus of an ape.

In the afternoon, a sheet of gray clouds covered the sky. Gusts of wind shook the coconut trees, blew papers, lifted the skirt of a white-haired old woman. It left me with the impression I was living in an imaginary world.

A flash of lightning split the sky and plunged into the sea, thunder bounced against the walls of the bathhouses and the bulk of the hotel. A reverberating blast, like the crushing of rocks in the sky.

These are the sounds of war, I thought, and I could not help but imagine an invasion rumbling like thunder, rending the island like a bolt of lightning burns across a patch of sky.

I can't make it fit together. The only feasible response for an insignificant man like myself is resignation. Thus did I clear my head, and I felt light and foolish.

Some people (they looked like foreigners) swam in the rain.

⸻ ⸻

Today I managed to attain a kind of pleasure in the dentists' drill, to realize that pain is not so menacing, that nothing bad will happen if I cease to resist it, and the dentist will be free to work on my cavities more easily. Pain is sweet.

It has been a month since I have touched these memoirs. I am writing them longhand now in a notebook. The racket of the typewriter bothers me. I remember the affidavit at the police station.

I spend hours leaning out the window; not hours, minutes; minutes in this day and age are equivalent to the hours of our grandparents who adopted the expression. I believe my grandparents spent their honeymoon in the Trotcha Hotel. I can see it perfectly from here. I feel I never really knew them, when I see the building and remember that the North American army used it during the first intervention.* In those days the Vedado must have been entirely in the country. Its contrast with the Riviera Hotel is most striking. The Trotcha is made of wood, one part, and the rest is colonial rubble masonry. It has just two floors, and the Riviera more than twenty, of concrete, almost windowless due to the air conditioning. Two eras, and both of them worthless.

On the sea is a small boat; it looks very small, because it is the only one to be seen across the entire horizon of blue and gray. On some of the roofs clothes are hung out to dry. Everything is so boring I don't know why I am describing it. Right now I'm looking at the little painting of Havana that we bought from Portocarrero; it is much more attractive than the city itself. It has more color; it is better composed. Havana doesn't have those colors. Havana is white, yellow, it's full of pale colors, washed out and dull: greens, blues, grays, pinks. Its buildings are of every type, not just colonial with balconies and heavy balustrades and stained glass windows and screens, like Portocarrero painted. He has caught what interests him about the city and painted the colors he has in his imagination. Everyone has a distinct city in his own mind.

For me, Havana is what I see from the window. It is the poplars of Vedado and the scraggly pines. The Trotcha is now a dilapidated boarding house; I see a woman sweeping in the wooden alcove, she has just moved the slatted shutters in order to sweep behind them. The balcony has those hanging wooden borders, something between icicles, snowflakes seen through a microscope and altar cloths embroidered by old aunts. But the wood looks gray, dirty and pockmarked.

On a tile roof clean clothes lie stretched out to dry, the blighted litter of man that pollutes and saddens everything. A child plays alone on a terrace; he has just spun to the floor after running around in circles. He got bored with running and threw himself on the ground.

Down the street, vehicles pass by and the people seem very small. I do not hear what they are saying. Nor do I care. I can imagine it.

What does all this mean? Why describe these things? I'm going to my study. What sense can be made of these roofs, the sea, the stretched out clothes, of people walking in the streets, the antiquated buildings, the new buildings, the children playing, the palm trees and the green poplars?

Noemí brought me a stack of photographs today. She said she'd had the time, that she'd meant to show them to me, but she had always forgotten them. "Could it be because you felt embarrassed?" I asked her, and she blushed. They are photos from the day they baptized her in the river. It is not how I imagined it. Nothing is. The white clothes do not cling to her body. Nor had I thought about the people; there are lots of people. The witnesses that are always everywhere.

I looked for her name in the Bible. She is the mother-in-law of Ruth. Noemí, my own; she ought to have advised herself instead of counseling Ruth: "lie down at his feet."

⸻ ⸻

The radio was playing on the other side of the bed; I couldn't turn it off without abandoning for a moment the warmth of Noemí. I thought about asking her to embrace me, and then I would roll over to the other side of the bed, stretch out my arm and shut off the radio. But no, anything might break the spell of the moment. I was even less willing to get up and return to bed after shutting off the music. Even the most insignificant gesture could spoil everything. The music didn't bother me as much as the voice of the singer, he made me feel like he was sitting with us here on the bed, and that afflicted me. I couldn't concentrate completely on Noemí.

It had been natural and sweet from the moment I approached her and kissed her eyes; she closed her eyelids, invisible when her eyes were open. I caught her eyelashes between my lips. That was downstairs in the living room.

The static of the North American radio station also was annoying, the station I casually tuned in so that nothing would be harsh, everything would be sweet, as sweet as it already was for me. For more than a year I had desired her. Her body was light; I had known it already, as if she had air in her bones like birds. As light as the first whore I held in my arms, adolescent and foolish. Above all, Noemí believed in God. I felt young.

I told this to her. "You don't know how I suffered every time I made your bed," she told me. "Don't laugh at me but many times I dreamed we were living together in this house and that was enough, I thought I would never have more than that, to dream that I embraced you and you came inside me." Her words mingled with the song: *I hate to see that evening sun go down, I hate to see that evening sun go down, 'cause my baby has gone left this town.* I tried to imagine it was Noemí's voice that sang, that it was her voice and not some alien voice. *Feeling tomorrow just like I feel today. Feeling tomorrow just like I feel today. I'm going to pack my troubles...*Everything is fine, even the song; I would always hum it tunelessly when I felt a melancholy happiness. It was a song of poor people, like Noemí, of careworn negroes. Everything, however, was fine.

I moved slowly, our labored breathing mingled with the hoarse alcoholic voice of the recording. "The music bothers me; I want to have you all to myself," I tell her with my arms propped on either side beside her shoulders, looking at her from above her body in the semi-darkness. "You have me," she answered. In love, every stupidity is precious. "I don't know what he is singing."

I remember the precise instant they suspended the song. Noemí raised her head, with the tips of her hair, short, disordered and blacker than the dark back of the bed, scarcely touching the sheets, and she kissed me tenderly. *Aggressive conduct, if allowed unchecked and unchallenged, ultimately leads to war...*

"Who is speaking?" Noemí asked after stopping me a few moments later. "It is Kennedy, I think…" I can never retain anything, but I remember these words: *I have directed...initial steps be taken immediately...a strict quarantine on all offensive military equipment...continued and increased close surveillance of Cuba and its military buildup...It shall be the policy of this nation to regard any nuclear missile launched from Cuba . . as an attack by the Soviet Union on the United States requiring full retaliatory response upon the Soviet Union . . Now your leaders are no longer Cuban leaders . . they are puppets and agents of an international conspiracy . . Your lives and lands are being used as pawns by those who deny you freedom...*Something like that. And other horrible words.

"What is he saying?" I stared fixedly at the frayed light on the dial of the radio. "I don't know. He says there are Russian rockets in Cuba." "What are those, my love?" she asked, embracing me, but now I did not feel anything. I was numb. "The atomic bomb?" "Yes, the atomic bomb," I told her. "He says they have proof, photographs. He says…I suppose the *yanquis* will invade us, the marines, they will bomb Havana first. I can't believe it, rockets here, in our pretty little Cuba." Noemí let go her embrace and cried: "Shit!"

We remained for a minute staring at the ceiling. Slices, circles and splinters of light entered through various cracks from the half-open shutters. Swords of light moved across the flat sky, and the cars passing in the streets below could be heard more clearly than ever, especially the air brakes of the buses.

It was all over. Good things always come late, when they no longer can be enjoyed. Noemí at my side, and I could feel no tenderness, only terror. Instead of feeling her skin, I felt her ribs, her lungs inflating and deflating with difficulty. We were naked in the bed, defenseless, two hairless animals, without powerful muscles, without protection, destitute. Sensuality had been converted to sadness. I felt ridiculous totally naked in bed, scared to death, my lungs heaving with anguish. Her little breasts, Noemi's black nipples beside me threw me into confusion.

I write in vain. Everything meaningless. Nothing has happened, but I feel asphyxiated. People talk and move about—I've just returned from a walk in the streets—as if war were a game. I have seen the German cities after the war. Ruins like decayed molars in Berlin and Hamburg. Little insignificant people drawing breath amid the debris. People mutilated. The hunger and fear and pettiness of men. They don't know what can happen to them. They're fools. They have an admirable serenity. I write to distract myself, to see if I can breathe a little easier. I look at the things in my apartment, and they tell me nothing.

I only spent a month in Germany after the war. It was towards the end of 1947; I had dollars on me, and it made me a king. But I didn't enjoy it; what was there to enjoy! I didn't understand anything. I was twenty-four years old and in love. I was running away from Hanna, and I felt like shit, a Jew on his way to the crematorium. I tried to put aside my memories. Who could go to bed with a German woman who lived in a half-ruined house, nearly destitute of food, with a brother who died in the war? Everyone had an egregious story to tell, but real. Everything was all mixed up. The first shock, I will never forget it, it's branded indelibly in my head. I was walking down the street, and I threw a cigarette butt to the ground. At once, three or four fellows lunged to the ground to recover it; I don't even know where they came from. It was an American cigarette. I turned scarlet red. Even a heavy set fellow with a suit and tie lunged to grab it, a respectable type, a German *herr professor,* and he dove to retrieve that butt, with a leather valise in his hand and all. I was embarrassed to watch them. I raised my head, I remember well, and I saw these ruins: a house without a roof and only two walls spotted with soot, green, like those with the rococo wreaths around the ceiling.

If they stop the Soviet ships that are on their way…We have atomic bombs! Cuba, with rockets! I can't even imagine it. One can imagine a rifle shot, a thrust of a knife, the explosion of a grenade. I cannot imagine the city of Havana destroyed, vaporized by a hydrogen bomb. They wouldn't drop a bomb here, because it could poison the air in Florida. I feel like cows on the farm during a rainstorm. They stand immobilized in the middle of the field.

Everything that enters my head is nonsense next to the facts. I feel everything is out of proportion. Cuba and the rest of the world. Nuclear energy and my little apartment. Everything is out of proportion. "We will ex-ter-mi-nate them," said Fidel, a short while ago. He grabbed the bull by the horns. He is prepared for anything. He is mad. I felt for a moment as he spoke, that he took the only position we can adopt. We stand at the summit of the world; we are not underdeveloped. Now I'm back to feeling stupid again, insignificant…I let myself get carried away. Others are deciding my life. I can do nothing. I control nothing. If I lie down to sleep, I may never get up again.

"We acquire the arms that we wish to acquire…and we take the measures we consider necessary for our defense…What are they?

We do not have to answer to the imperialists…No one is going to inspect our country. No one will enter our country to inspect it, because we will never give that authority to anyone, we will never renounce our sovereign right that inside our borders we are the ones who make the decisions, we are the ones who inspect and no one else…Whoever intends to inspect Cuba needs to know that they must come prepared for combat!.. If they form a blockade, they are going to exalt our country, because our country will steadfastly resist…We are part of humankind, and we accept these risks, but we are not afraid. We must know how to live in this epoch in which we have been chosen to live and we must know how to live with dignity. All of us, men and women, young and old, we are all one in this hour of danger!" We are all one; I will die the same as the rest. This island is a trap, and the revolution is a tragedy, a tragedy because we are too small to survive or triumph. Too few and too poor. It is a very expensive dignity. I do not want to think about it. I remember each of Fidel's phrases with clarity, even the tone, I read it twenty times to fill the vacuum, to try to relax, and now I want to forget the whole thing. I want to get lost. Disappear. I am going mad. I do not want to know anything. I do not want to remember. I do not want to have an inconsolable memory.

I went outside, I came back. I cannot endure either my house or the street. On the *malecón* the waves slop against the sea wall. An island is a trap, the revolution caught us all here inside it; to stare out at the sea brought no relief. You couldn't see anything; I thought I saw gray battleships and aircraft carriers floating by, grazing my face. They will certainly bomb us first, soften us up and destroy us, but the sky was silent, and I was still alive. The security of the moment was meaningless; it was a moment without a future. This moment also is without future. Everything might suddenly burst into "billowing flames" and "radiant light," as the monstrous description I just read says about the hydrogen bomb. Nothing is happening. And everything is possible.

I walked and walked, and suddenly I felt a roar approaching the wide boulevard. The roar seemed to engulf the entire city. Tanks began to rumble past, trucks towing cannons, cannons, indistinct shapes of an incomprehensible size, and a long flatbed, almost without end, a dark canvas covering everything, something very big. My knees buckled under me, I feared another arrest; at night by the *malecón*; they would accuse me of spying; I didn't even watch, I only heard the roar. I decided it was a rocket, a highly combustible explosive; that we would all be blown away. I felt a blow on my leg, I jumped; I bent down and picked up a piece of asphalt. The procession was ripping out shards of asphalt in the darkness. I kept walking. The last cannons lumbered past pointing at the road they left behind with me.

Above, the stars lit insignificant specks in the sky, now dark. The stars offer comfort to no one. They ignore us from far away. They are totally indifferent. They have nothing to do with us. So much romantic shit has the revolution destroyed!

To think about bombardments and invasions, blood and cadavers, stinking, mutilated, rotten, is worse than accepting atomic destruction. Yes, I would prefer that everything burst suddenly in a brilliant light, be devoured or evaporated by billowing flames, than lose a leg, or bleed slowly in the streets. To die by the work of a clean bomb, as Eisenhower called it. A clean bomb, without much radioactive filth left around. Before, I believed it was a macabre and foolish idea, but now it comforts me, it is a splendid idea, a clean death, without pain or blood.

Another large sledge passed like a train carrying another massive bulk covered with a dark and oily canvas. I thought I saw a hand saluting me.

Now we are a modern country, we have 20th century weapons, atomic bombs, rockets; no longer are we an insignificant colony, today we have entered history, we possess the same weapons as Russia and the United States. Our power to destroy makes us the equal for a moment of the two great powers. They will not tolerate us, I am sure, they will seize our arms, they will disregard us; they will obliterate the island.

I've heard nothing from Noemí. Will she come tomorrow? I don't care about tomorrow. I cannot love anyone; everything is incapacitated. I am impotent to desire her. Life has stopped, I must let everything go: the world has opened up beneath my feet, I sink into the void, I go insane.

I could not sleep last night. I turn again to the street. A north wind blows, very violent. The waves break and leap above the wall, they break against the trucks and autos, against the grillwork and pitted walls of the façades. The air is saturated with water. It is cold. All around us explosions of water are hurled, spraying pieces of wood all over the street. I saw a butterfly on a vacant lot, and I felt as though everything suddenly had stopped because the world was going to end at this very moment. Aloft in the air, it seemed suspended, dead. On the street I felt worse, more vulnerable. Walking did not resolve anything. Greater danger hovers in the street. There is nothing I can do, nothing I can change. I am a victim. I cannot explain it, but seeing that butterfly made me feel more terrified than I have ever felt, and I don't know why.

The telephone rang, it appeared to be long distance, and when I picked up the receiver I heard a strange conversation. "I didn't tell her anything, she doesn't know anything. She saw a lot of people rushing around in the hospital." A masculine voice was speaking, the woman insisted: "Didn't she ask you anything?" "When they set the wooden tables in the corridor to lay corpses, it's scary, Irene, tables with I.D. card and string, labels to tag and tie to the ankles of the wounded, the dead, with a number, a name or something, the nurses told me; when she saw the tables, yes, she asked about them." "What did you tell her?" "I told her it was a cyclone. There had been a cyclone." "Yes, she will understand that much better, she saw cyclones in '26 and '44, but she has never seen a war." "You haven't either." "Are you afraid?" "They will have to kill me." "Don't say that, for the sacred heart of Jesus, you only provoke the devil." "Neither God nor the devil exist, I'm a revolutionary, revolutionaries don't believe in religious superstitions." "You should at least have some respect..." "Liberty or death! We shall prevail!" He began to shout. I stopped listening and hung up the phone. It's the only violent reaction I've heard during this whole period. People in general are too serene.

The phone rang again, again the prolonged rings of long distance, but when I picked it up, nobody was there, just the hollow drone of the telephone. Could it be Laura or my parents trying to call me from New York? I won't answer. I don't want to talk to anybody. I have nothing to say, what am I going to tell them? I don't want to know anything about anybody.

After hanging up the phone, I went to the kitchen and took out a little rice from the refrigerator, but I couldn't swallow it, the cold grains of rice would not go down my throat.

I would like, I would like so many things. I wish I were in the sky. The earth offends me. I would like to be in a plane, from any country, a MIG or a U2. It is all the same to me.

I want to grab hold of everything, and I don't care about anything. I don't know what I am doing. I just put my thumb in my mouth and began to strike my thumbnail against the edge of my teeth. For some minutes. My thumb came out dragging a thread of clear saliva. I thought for a moment I was being observed; I turned around, but no one was there. I dried my finger mechanically on the coarse fabric of my pants.

I want to write it all down. Everything I do seems remarkable. I pulled from the pocket of my wrinkled shirt a blue and white pack of cigarettes, Virginia tobacco, Dorados. I took out a cigarette and tapped it vehemently against the table. The green head of the match ignited in flame and I almost burn my fingers. I inhale and absorb a mouthful of warm smoke. I look at the point of ash in the ashtray, the white paper. I grab the cigarette, exhale the smoke above the table, the books, the papers. A fleck of tobacco falls on the table.

I look at the floor and see a wastebasket, with hair and cobwebs and dirt, behind the bookshelf.

I went to bed and turned the light off, but I cannot sleep. The rockets are there, in Pinar del Rio, Santa Clara, Oriente…It seems the island has rockets on every corner. They will wipe us off the map; they will send us to the alligators at the bottom of the Caribbean. Afterwards the ships will float over us, and they will say: "This is where Cuba used to be." And waves and currents will sweep the island buried at the bottom of the sea.

By now the Pentagon should have completed its plan to destroy us. They will flatten us simply with the number of their arms and men. And if the Russians fire off their rockets the world probably will be split in two. All for the island of Cuba. We've never been more important or more miserable. To fight against the United States has grandeur, but I don't want that destiny. I prefer to remain a backward country. I am not interested, or attracted to a destiny that must confront death every minute in order to survive. The revolutionaries are the mystics of the 20th century: they are prepared to die for an implacable social justice. I am a mediocrity, a modern man, a link in the chain, an insignificant cockroach.

Every sound anticipates the end of the world. An auto passing down the street, a coughing motor, a door slamming. All these sounds are like the beginning of the end. I cannot imagine atomic destruction; it is something completely unfathomable to me. I don't know how to understand the event. I will turn to ash, to dust, to vapor. It is worthless to protest: I live here and will die with the rest. Everyone is fucked alike. I see myself among the ruins of Vedado, transformed into a mist…

I don't want to sleep; nor do I wish to stay here. I want a glass of water; I'll eat something; not even that. If I go out to the street it will be worse, seeing people. What am I doing? What good does it do to fight it like this?

Easy, easy.

And yet, I don't want to die, I still cling to that foolish hope of breaking free, of being happy some day. Bullshit. I'll never learn. Now, now is the only time I have.

Why? I am afraid of losing my bullshit personality, my memories, my desires, my sensations.

This diary is useless.

Underdevelopment and civilization. I'll never learn.

I take myself too seriously.

Everything I am saying is something that festers inside me, sinks deep within my flesh. I probe. I track it down. Go away. Get out of here.

If they do not drop the bomb, if we survive. My head. I don't care. It doesn't matter to me. Lies. It all matters to me.

And if the bombing should start right now?

Everything would be blown to hell. I am tangled up again. Rage, rage. To what purpose. Why write a question mark. Periods. Letters.

Let go, let go, let go. Not even that. My head is a trap. I am ensnared. Thinking. It separates me from everything. Me, me, nothing. I track it down, there, and there and there. Everything makes me suffer, and the thing is it does not exist.

I am going to die, and soon. It's all right; I accept it. I will not try to hide in the cracks like a cockroach. There are no cracks anymore. The cracks and holes and refuges are all gone.

The October Crisis is over. The Crisis of the Caribbean. To name enormous things is to kill them. Words are small, paltry things. If I had died, everything would have ended. But I am still alive. And to still be alive is also to destroy the moment of its intense profundity. (How false these words!)

I want to keep my vision of the days of the crisis clear and clean. The events, the fear, the yearning suffocate me. It's hard. Aside from that, I have nothing more to add. I will stop here. Mankind (I) is sad, but it wants to live.

To live beyond words.

APPENDICES

Jack and the Fare Collector

———

"*Please, does this bus take me to the beach?*" asked Jack, his blue eyes opening wider behind his spectacles.

"Move aside," instructed a woman in a white uniform, brushing Jack's legs with a bag full of avocados.

"Okay, let's hit it!" and the fare collector struck the bell three times, then punched a sharp final ring.

"Por favoar, *does this bus take me to the beach?*"

The fare collector stepped in front of Jack with his palm extended: "That'll be eight centavos, *fiy cen*...Where do you want to go? I do not *espeaki ingli*."

"Chico, *I want to go to the beach*, acua; *you know*." Jack pronounced each word very slowly. "*For Christ's sake, and I had Spanish for two years back in school. You know...All I can remember is* acua*, water...I'm probably pronouncing it wrong . . You tengo un lapis, that's I have a pencil. No good.*"

"I don't understand, *amigo*," exclaimed the fare collector and, turning his head toward the seated passengers, he shouted, "I don't know what this American wants."

"*Don't* amigo *me, you know very well what I'm asking you, I want to go to the beach.*"

"*Meester, you wan guman,*" said a frail-looking man standing next to the fare collector, one hand clutching the overhead rail. His white shirt hung down over his pants, tight at the ankles.

"*Oh, drop dead!*"

"Anybody here know English?" cried a voice seated behind the driver.

"*This is too much!*" exclaimed Jack, adjusting his glasses and running his hand across his chestnut brown hair. "*Stop the bus, I'm getting off*"—and a magazine fell from his arm. On a glossy page pressed against the dusty floor a red lipstick draws near a pale, disembodied mouth, its lips parted in a sensual "o".

"DON'T SHOUT AT ME! I'm not here to carry your bags. I don't get paid to know English."

"*Oh go to hell, you are all the same, ignorant bastards!*"

"The ignoramus would be you!"

"Let him get off and find somebody who knows English," cried a voice from the middle of the bus.

"*I better get off,*" and Jack stepped down a stair to the door. "*He'll never understand me.*"

"Good riddance!" exclaimed the fare collector, ringing his bell violently; the cord leaping between the eyelets. "If I knew English I wouldn't be working a bus."

"Where did that American want to go?" asked a man as he withdrew his head from the window. "Maybe this bus is what he wanted."

"Right away the guy starts shouting at me..."

"He's a foreigner, *chico*," said a surly voice.

"Foreigners, Cubans, everybody thinks they are in the right and all conductors are idiots. That's not so bad. What's worse for us is we have to scrape and bow to the public, people like you, all day long."

"That boy was right to have been so nervous; imagine what it is like to get on a bus in Cuba and not know how to speak Spanish."

"Nobody is right; everybody is wrong."

Believe It or Not

She smiled stiffly, her lips carefully painted, her skin smooth, her clear eyes looking off to one side—while the dark-complexioned old man, one enormous ear, his nose against her white cheek, a blurred half-closed eye—kissed her stiffly.

The photo fell to the ground.

Eduardo stooped grunting and picked it up. In here he looks like a chimpanzee, he thought, but in the others he looks like a fetus. When he is by himself, he looks like a fetus.

He pressed the tab key on the typewriter three times with his thumb…the Chief Editor insisted and Eduardo agreed to interview the old man, Javier Pereira. He thought it was a good opportunity to spend a few hours outside the office. An expedition by *Ripley's Believe It or Not* had just discovered him in the Colombian Andes.

When he arrived with the photographer at the Manhattan Towers Hotel, they were cutting Pereira's hair. The wrinkled figure had sunk his head in his chest, entranced, while the barber passed the clippers smoothly along his neck. Eduardo noticed uneven tufts of sandy hair on the towel that covered his shoulders; he imagined that the barber was picking fleas.

By a half-open door he saw two men eating in the next room. A nurse in white starched uniform whirled about the suite. Probably to make an impression, Eduardo thought, to cast a scientific air on the matter. That night they would present the old Colombian on television. The entire United States would have the opportunity to see him without leaving their houses or tossing down drinks in some bar.

"Emilio, take a photo of him like that," said Eduardo to his Puerto Rican photographer.

After the first flash of light, the barber asked if he would sell him a photo:

"It's just what I was looking for. A wonderful conversation piece. It's the type of thing I like to put in a frame and hang in the barbershop…you know, for the clients," and he shook the towel in a corner of the salon. Irregular tufts of straw-colored hair fell about the polished oak floor, between the wall and green carpet.

The nurse approached with a cup of coffee and she put it in the hands of the old man. Pereira began to drink the coffee mechanically, spilling a little upon the wide tie he wore to his trousers.

"Take him drinking coffee," said his manager entering the room with a napkin in his hand. "Isn't he amazing! You may not believe it, but the old man grew up drinking coffee his whole life. Did you know that? Drinking Colombian coffee. *It's the best damn coffee in the world."*

The head full of wrinkles whistled each time it slithered the liquid between its false teeth. Emilio crouched down and snapped another shot.

"The old man is strong as a bull," said his manager, wiping his meaty lips with the unfolded napkin. He wore a shiny suit of Italian silk. He looked indecisively at the napkin and opened the drawer of a table beneath an enormous mirror and concealed it. He shoved the drawer closed with a slap.

The old man continued to drink his coffee while looking at the manager.

*"Poor thing…*They ought to give you something to eat, something special. Pablum for babies or something" said the newspaperman who had just entered the room.

Surely he is on a diet, Eduardo thought looking at the tailored suit, he is a woman about to wither away. Shriveled to a wisp.

"Don't let him fool you," said the manager taking a toothpick from his pocket and putting it in his mouth. "He is stronger than a bull. He eats everything. You should see him eating an ice cream."

He swore that Javier Pereira was 167 years old. A team of doctors at City Hall had just finished giving him a general examination and they had declared the old man without a shadow of a doubt to be at least 150 years of age.

Emilio sat down on a chair, his half-closed eyes fixed on Eduardo. He didn't think; he only did what he was told. That way he got along with everybody.

Several newspapermen entered and two photographers; the room was illuminated with explosions of light...The old man got up angrily and tried to punish the closest photographer, who backed away before he could grab him. The old man kept waving his arms in the air.

"Bastards, don't take any more photos, goddamn it."

"*What does he say?*" asked the newspapermen.

"He speaks *maquiritare*," said the manager, "an indigenous dialect nearly unknown, but we have brought an interpreter with us, a doctor Gerard. Doctor Gerard has studied the indigenous languages of Colombia for many years."

What arrogance! thought Eduardo; I won't say anything. To expose the manager would be to desecrate the event; apparently he hadn't heard Eduardo tell him that he worked for *La Prensa*, the Spanish-speaking paper in New York.

The doctor tamped a pinch of tobacco with his thumb, approached the group, lit his smoke and extinguished the match in the air. He sucked a few times on his pipe:

"*He says that only the sun can shine like that on his face.* The Indians from that part of the Andes where we discovered Javier worship the sun above all other things."

In a corner of the room, the manager and doctor Gerard talked with the newspapermen and stole glances at one another in the enormous mirror.

Eduardo drew near the old man:

"Don't you feel strange here? Don't you miss Colombia?"

"When I was in Cartagena I saw a sight, what a sight!"

The old man waved his hands in the air trying to erase the room in order to recreate the panorama of Cartagena; gray ruins and sea.

"I have a lot of money," he said, pounding with his open hand the pocket of his jacket. Then he took out a wallet of imitation leather and extracted some quantity of Colombian pesos and a five-dollar bill.

"Photos are no good . . You cannot buy anything with photos. I have a lot of money," and he concealed the wallet back inside his jacket.

"How long have you been here?" Eduardo asked. It never occurred to him to ask something intelligent in his interviews.

"I have been here two months. Tomorrow I go back."

"I thought you had only arrived yesterday."

"No, it's been two months."

"All right," said Eduardo without believing the old man, remembering that the manager intended to take him around the country before returning him to Colombia.

The manager approached, taking the arm of the newspaperman. It had occurred to him to photograph the old man with the beak-nosed blonde. She smiled.

"*The beauty and the beast!*" exclaimed the manager. "La bella y la bestia!"

The blonde brushed her hand across his face smiling. The old man pushed her. He thought the blonde was going to steal his wallet. He grabbed his pocket with his hand. At last he agreed to the photo.

"*He's so cute*," she repeated in order to convince him. "He is so nice, such a sweet little monkey."

The old man put his arm around her waist and the woman returned a smile. He kissed her on the cheek. At that moment Eduardo felt a convulsion in his eyes from the venomous brilliance of the cameras.

"Put me in a bed with her," cried the old man.

Emilio smiled and then became very serious.

They separated the pair and the old man began to whirl about the room.

"I'm getting out of here...."

Eduardo did not return that afternoon to his paperwork at the offices of the magazine. Emilio, after loaning the old man his wristwatch, left to develop his pictures. I forgot to ask him, thought Eduardo as he crossed Central Park on foot, why he had loaned him the watch. He looked at the profile of the skyscrapers at the end of the park and he considered that Pereira was more than six thousand kilometers from the Andes.

Eduardo bent and read again the magazine clipping lying on

the table. He wanted to finish his article for the Sunday supplement with the words of the Colombian lawyer who claimed ownership of Javier Pereira. He had initiated a lawsuit against Ripley's. His client was a landholder from Medellín who professed that the old man belonged to him because he lived on his property.

On a very white page, Eduardo typed in large print. TO WHOM DOES THE OLD MAN BELONG? He crossed it out with a string of x's. Then he wrote: MORE THAN 167 YEARS OF DRINKING COFFEE AND HE STILL LIKES BLONDES.*

---

*Pereira died some months after returning to Colombia. He died and they buried him, and they even have a postage stamp with the profile of the old man.

Yodor

⸺◦⸺

I have something to show you; I mean—here it is, if you've got a moment…I can come back later.

Maybe it will; it might interest you. I don't know.

They didn't believe me yesterday. I started to tell them you know—how I built Yodor. And the national and international repercussions it had; it's all there, I'm not making it up. You can read it right there in those newspaper clippings. My parents about died of a heart attack when they saw him speaking in my own voice.

They didn't believe me. It's not their fault; anyone who looks at me thinks I've been a dip shit my whole life, someone incapable of creating a marvel like Yodor.

And this, it isn't the whole thing. I had a much more complete album, but the American lost it who tried to bring Yodor to the United States. Yodor's main ambition was to walk the streets of New York. If only they had let him stroll down 5th Avenue!

Roberto saw Yodor in Parque Colón, I exhibited him there; his father took him; he remembered as soon as he saw the photographs.

No, no; the other Roberto. The cabinetmaker didn't say anything. The draftsman, the one who works with me.

Even though Roberto is the one who called me a liar yesterday.

He talked, he walked, he smoked. You'll see for yourself later when you read the clippings. No, no; but I was actually commended by a conference of radio technicians that was meeting in Havana at that time. I constructed, you can see me here, the first robot in the world that walked.

You're making fun of me…No, no; it doesn't bother me. I'm used to it. Even my wife. We never speak of Yodor.

You'll see how it all came about. I'm always thinking when I'm working at my desk. For years I thought about this. I was artistic director for a magazine here, I don't know if you remember it, it was very famous in the 20's, *Metropolitan*. You know it? That's the one. I was the artistic director and one day they offered me the chance to work in New York as a draftsman at a public relations agency. I worked time and a half every day and they paid me; they paid me for the extra time. I didn't have anything to do in New York; there were a lot of people, sure, but I didn't know anybody. I left a wife and two children here. One day while drawing and thinking absent-mindedly it occurred to me to do something remarkable, something that no one had done before, something that would attract people like flies. You can't know what it meant, back in 1930, I'm telling you, to come out with a mechanical puppet that could walk, talk and smoke!

Not at all. I didn't think at all about science or discoveries. Yodor was a remarkable device that could advertise anything. That's what I believed. People would go to look at the robot, ask him things, and then the puppet, between one answer and another—pam!— out would slip a promotion for a pack of cigarettes, a drink. Anything. It was a different kind of advertising.

Me. Just me. I didn't consult with anybody.

I returned from New York with three thousand pesos saved. That amount is nothing today. Back then it was some big-time cash. With that money I could have started a business, even a business like this furniture store. I had a single idea in my head: Yodor, Yodor, Yodor. I thought about what the puppet would be like and I trembled with a strange emotion. My wife wanted to buy a house in El Vedado. All I saw in front of me was the robot. I had thousands of drawings. I had to do it. If I didn't do it, I would explode.

But I didn't tell anyone about it! For years afterwards I told no one about Yodor. I didn't tell them, besides, because I thought no one would be interested. That's the truth.

Yes, that's me twenty years ago. You don't recognize me? I was in all the papers. Even *La Semana Cómica*. You'll see the caricature in a minute. They used to say that Batista manipulated his ministers and even the President from behind the scenes; in those days I think it was Laredo Brú,* Bururú, they called him...Allow me, let me find it for you. See there; they put the body of Yodor with the head of the ministers. Careful, the pages are very old and they will tear very easily. Batista manipulated his ministers like I, unseen, manipulated Yodor. Batista hasn't changed. I have. I have crumbled back to dust, and he still sticks to the hog. The robot went to hell. Now nobody remembers Yodor.

Nonsense. I never got involved with politics. Whenever anyone asked Yodor a political question, he would change the subject and talk about sports. That's right, he knew a lot about sports. You think I'm an idiot? If he had spoken of politics in those days they would have beat him to a pulp. Or beat me to a pulp, same thing. They would have ripped me to shreds, no question. Same as now.

I spent more than two years constructing the robot. And meanwhile I kept working for *Metropolitan*. Piece by piece. I had to design him from top to toe. I started by drawing out each detail; the hardest part was the articulation of the legs. You've got to realize the puppet weighed a ton; he had a gyroscope to keep his equilibrium. The same principle as the gyroscope. A true automaton has to walk; if he doesn't, he isn't an automaton.

When one piece didn't work, I had to manufacture another one. I designed exactly what I needed, and I went over to a shop on Avocado Street. I filled our bedroom with parts and apparatus. Finally my wife and I had no more room in our apartment. The three of us didn't fit. We had to leave and let Yodor have the bedroom to himself. We slept in the living room.

Although she didn't like it. You don't know the price I had to pay. I realize it now, but while I was constructing him I thought of nothing else. Everything was for Yodor.

You've got to realize it was I alone, right here in Cuba, with no knowledge or very little of radio mechanics, who gave to the world the first fully automated robot. It's the truth. In the whole world, there was nothing like it.

Now they even sell them in the toy stores, for children. Last year I bought one for my granddaughter, one of the Three Kings, Robie it was called, but my wife, as soon as she saw it, threw it out.

I don't know where she put it; she disappeared it. I even looked in the garbage. It cost me 15 pesos.

Exactly right, a Frankenstein; that's what I made, you said it right; I created a Frankenstein.

I made it up. I can invent a ton of names, just like Yodor. I have a facility for creating names. You don't believe it? Would you like me to invent some names on the spot? Here they are from nothing: *Aisú, Chócolo, Belba, Leimo, Tranquisuto, Pla, Nicelina, Cateca, Tuturaca, Chojú, Ninnán, Chechujo, Tincatún*…I could invent names like this for hours and hours. They come to me on their own accord. Sometimes without realizing, it, I begin to give strange names to things. You can be sure I never call this the "furniture store," I always call it the box yard.

No. I don't know. I can't explain it. My daughter, I don't know why, I always call her *Ompica*. *Ompica* over here, *Ompica* over there, and I don't know where I got that name. Verbs, also, like *racionalipichar, gatar, yoder, venchar, rochelear*….

I presented my first exhibition for my parents. They're dead now; back then they were both getting very old. I sat them down in the living room without telling them anything and I left. By remote control I had Yodor leave the bedroom and walk to the living room. No, no; that wasn't what frightened them. At first they started to laugh…

I know because my wife was with them and she told me afterwards.

But, as soon as Yodor began to speak they were struck with alarm. When they heard the puppet speak with my own voice they started to cry: "Get out of there, Paco, get out of there!" I am on the terrace roof and I hear the cries. I told them to calm down but they wouldn't. They threw themselves on the monster and tried to yank him to the floor by his tinplate arms. My mother ended up with Yodor in a bear hug. I had to race down from the terrace.

That was when it occurred to me to open a peephole in his chest, you don't see it, there you can see it in the photograph, so people would not think there was a person inside. That's why I put that little window there.

You don't know what those little holes are for? Clustered in a star. The amplifier, that's where the voice comes from.

Another day I invited the press. Only three or four newspaper-men came. Even though I'd sent invitations to all the papers. At first they were a little wary. They thought I had a cat trapped inside. Then to finish the exhibition Yodor went down the stairs, I lived on a first floor, and he walked down the stairs. He even crossed the street. At once he raised a commotion, and I had to take him to the house.

Yes. But only once. A little hellion from the neighborhood; that happened much later, because at first they thought Yodor was a su-perman. Many of the kids there would run away from him when he came down the stairs. But like everything else: they lost respect for him. They realized he could not hurt them. This ruffian I am telling you about, the son of Chiqui, my wife's best friend, tripped him one day and naturally he fell scared to death in the street.

No. Nothing happened to him. A little dent on a flank. Nothing important. I gave him a little dab of aluminum paint and he was good as new. Oh yes, I began to keep watch over the robot, over the people that hung around, because once they got over their fear, they would always dream about doing some mischief. It's like when we were boys we lost respect for the priest and one day we made a bet be-tween us to see who would dare to throw a stone inside the church. We did it and nothing happened.

Yes, yes; very likely. Yodor is my penance. A penance a little brutish, a little extreme, because I didn't throw the stone, it was Tito. Tito was the hell raiser.

On the following week the newspapermen returned. They asked me to do another demonstration. Around twenty of them came this time, and they brought several engineers and radio technicians.

The next day it was in all the newspapers. Front page. You saw those clippings already; they are the first ones in the album. These here. Look.

I told myself: "Well, you have it made." My star was launched. Now came the sweet part, to harvest what had been seeded by my three years of work! At once I took Yodor to the Alfred Tobacco Company. They were very enthusiastic, especially when in the middle of the demonstration I'd set up, Yodor asked for a cigarette. I had to draw the light toward him, but as soon as he exhaled the bluish smoke they saw the robot's enormous advertising potential. The American who was watching everything said dying of laughter that it depended on what brand of cigarette Yodor smoked, because if he smoked Partagas the company was not interested. Then Yodor exclaimed: "I smoke only Chester, because it doesn't oxidize my throat."

The American wrote to the company. They responded at once, within a week, offering me ten thousand pesos a month for the exclusive rights to the robot. They promised to send me a one-year contract, for starters. I dreamed every night of Yodor walking through the streets of New York.

Why? I couldn't dream about another city; I didn't know any other city in the United States.

Then the other puppet showed up. The laboratories at Westinghouse had manufactured and patented a robot that also talked and smoked. They even sent me a photo of the other creature; it had some bullshit name, but I don't remember it. There it is.

That one there, Elmer, that's what they called it.

Do you see it? Look at it good...

I realized at once that Elmer was a cripple. He spent his life in a chair. He couldn't walk. I sent about ten letters explaining Yodor's superiority, the first robot in the world that walked. They answered me that they weren't in the business of selling shoes, but cigarettes.

I thought I would go to New York anyway. I was sure that, if I could speak with the people there—I wanted to show them Yodor's elegant grace—that I could convince the manufacturers of the superiority of my own creation. Then I found out there was a patent that protected the Westinghouse robot for five years against all competitors that knew how to smoke, even if they could walk. I had to wait five years to take Yodor up North!

Bullshit! What could I do with that! I thought nobody had a robot like him, that the world hadn't seen anything like it . . But no; I was knee-deep in shit; I was wrong. They'd screwed me good. So, here's Westinghouse, with a bunch of engineers, all the most advanced equipment, they didn't have to worry about money, and here I am, by myself, with three thousand dollars, without any title or anything, a poor Cuban from Güira de Melena, a draftsman, that's all I am, not studied, even so I made a robot that smokes and speaks like an American, and, above all, it walks.

What could I do? I began to give exhibitions over in Parque Colón. Also at the Campoamor Theater. But that didn't solve anything. You don't know what it cost me to maintain Yodor. More than a Congo slave. And I was the slave. I lived every day hanging on Yodor's needs. Every week some part broke down, they were so delicate and precise, and once again I'd have to draft a design and send it to a factory. Whatever the repair, it cost me a ton of money. The transportation…hell, just to move him from one place to another I had to rent a truck, remember it weighed a ton.

I'm going, don't worry, I'll go…I've bored you enough already. You sure?

In Cuba Yodor couldn't survive. At the time there were only two or three large companies here that could lease Yodor to advertise their business. With maintenance and transportation expenses, he cost about a thousand or fifteen hundred pesos a month. I offered to rent him for three thousand a month. I thought of Bacardi and Crusellas and Sobates, and that's it. I had almost convinced the people at Crusellas; they were about to sign the contract when Guastela put himself in the middle of things and botched up the negotiation. He filled their heads with bullshit; he told the people of Crusellas that for the same money he could wage a publicity campaign in the press and over the radio. Plus, a variety of spectacular programs in the Alcazar Theater. That was it for me, he ploughed my sales pitch into the ground. Afterwards he didn't do half the things he promised; and he made a lot of money. But Guastela had more facility with words, more contacts, and I only had Yodor.

Then I thought of renting him to two promoters. I had one, the Gravi company. Gravi toothpaste was interested, but I never found the second sponsor. I had to be content with taking him on tour around the island. I found a tumbledown truck, and I took off with an associate for the road.

A total success. In every town I went he was a sensation; I rented the best theater and put on one or two exhibitions.

It depended. A boisterous mob would gather when I arrived in town…

No, I had to ask the police for special permission. I went to see

General Ezequiel Piedra. I wanted permission to parade Yodor through the streets. The police had forbidden it after the two riots that happened in Prado. They told me that Yodor was a very problematic robot because he brought public disorder. I insisted that Yodor didn't know anything about politics. But he assured me that the enemies of the state utilized my "mechanical monkey" for their attacks against the government. He said he could not permit it. Then I really laid it on thick…I insinuated that the whole island of Cuba was anxious to see him, what would people think . . That's what I said, and I didn't offer him a penny. Finally he gave in, he gave me special permission to exhibit him in the parks and he put at my disposal two policemen in every town we appeared. "I don't know what people see in him," he told me afterwards when we took our leave, "I do everything that Yodor does and a lot more, and nobody pays money to see me."

Everywhere. Don't you see the programs? This is from Bayamo. In Oriente they took me to every corner, even over dirt roads. The truck was a pile of junk, and don't forget Yodor weighed about a ton. Still and all, I went to places a bristle brush won't reach. One time they set me up. They told me I could catch a dirt road, a narrow embankment where the truck could barely fit: and the road ended in a pasture. Without any warning, it disappeared right in the middle of a pasture. They said it was the shortest way. I think it was near Banes. We had already gone about five kilometers. We had to go back the whole way in reverse. I was behind with Yodor, giving instructions to my associate who was driving. I felt…I had never felt so miserable. I looked at the road and at Yodor completely covered with red dirt and I remembered that once I had dreamed of strolling with my robot down the streets of New York, with the people shouting and throwing confetti from skyscrapers, like in the news. Instead I was crawling backwards on a muddy road in the middle of a jungle, because it was a jungle, pure and simple. The only thing missing were the lions.

In every town, it's the truth, people filled the theaters. In the beginning, at some town in Havana province, Batabanó, I don't know, I don't remember; the fact is there was only one person in the theater, only one. It was the only time it happened to me.

No, how could I even think to cancel the program! I gave that fellow the best exhibition that Yodor gave in his whole life. He was clever that day. He walked up and down the stage, smoking and answering questions. That person left convinced that Yodor was a Martian. He talked about Mars as if he were an astronomer. I don't know, I think I might have read something in *Bohemia*; the fact is when the fellow asked Yodor why he was made of iron, he answered that on Mars there wasn't any water, that everything was iron, that nothing was flexible and smooth like on Earth. The fellow dropped his jaws. I'm sure he never in his life had witnessed a spectacle like that one. That was no spectacle; it was the real thing. That night even I believed Yodor was a Martian.

Later, I didn't know what to do with Yodor. Sure he was famous, the whole world knew about him, but I was busted. I didn't want to be famous or appear in the papers, all I wanted was to have money.

I ended up renting him for birthday parties. They hired me like they hired Mandrake the Magician and the clowns. I worked with people that couldn't earn a living in even the sleaziest circuses and shows. I swear, the children would laugh and joke more with Yodor than the clown.

I refused to take him out of the house. Then I ran into an American lawyer, a fellow who spoke excellent Spanish, who told me he would take Yodor's case to the courts. Even the U.S. Supreme Court, that's exactly what he said, if it was necessary. Yodor would have to march through the streets of Chicago, San Francisco, Washington...He's the one who lost the album I'd been filling with all the things that had been published about Yodor; I even had the transcripts from the radio programs. It had everything, the whole nine yards. I lost it. What you see there doesn't amount to even half the things that happened to Yodor.

I gave some exhibitions in the house from time to time, just to keep him in shape. But we lived on the first floor and the house shook with such force whenever Yodor walked that the neighbors complained to the owner of the house. Now I hardly ever took Yodor from his room. We slept in the living room, and Yodor completely took over our bedroom. I always left him standing there bewildered in front of the mirror.

The last time he went out was because the priests of the school at Belén came to ask about him, they begged me to bring him to a raffle they were going to have; I don't know what for, I think to raise money for the missions or the parochial schools, some such crap.

One day my wife told me angrily: "And to think you've spent three thousand pesos in order to make that piece of shit." She said it with fury.

The robot doesn't exist any longer. I hacked it to pieces. One day I grabbed an axe and I ripped it apart. I destroyed it.

No, no; I threw away the pieces little by little. The garbage men refused to take the whole thing at one time. Every day I threw a few pieces in the garbage can.

Yes, I know that other people try to do the same thing and fail. But for me fame is not important. I was famous for a year, and so what? Look at me now. Did you ever once think that I, Paco Torres, was capable of constructing the first robot in the world that walked?

Yodor was a very big deal for Cuba, very expensive; he was a puppet beyond remuneration.

NOTES

*Page 20

The provocative sexiness of women…one of the principal causes of the decay and death of the spirit.

*Page 21

Philosophy of life

*Page 21

It is quite obvious to me that I have always been of an inferior race. I don't understand rebellion. My race has never rebelled except to plunder: to devour like wolves a beast they did not kill.

*Page 23

Reconcentración. To help put down the Cuban insurrection in 1896, Spain decreed that the rural population be evacuated from the countryside and relocated to specifically designated fortified towns. Peasants were herded into these reconcentration camps. Their villages and fields were burned, and their livestock was seized. The overcrowded concentration centers became breeding grounds for disease, sickness and ultimately mass deaths.

*Page 26

I desired to have an inconsolable memory.

*Page 34

Colloquially, "change" or "agitation." For José Ortega y Gasset, *"alteración"* is a term of art meaning the state of being governed by things outside oneself, of responding to stimulus without premeditation. Animals, as opposed to humans, are *"pura alteración,"* because they have no self with which to confront the world.

*Page 64

that gracious spot, set between firm and fleshy thighs, within its little garden plot …the garden, foul!

*Page 78

The five-year military occupation of Cuba by the United States after the Spanish-American War (1898-1902). Subsequent interventions were sanctioned by a codicil to the 1902 Cuban constitution known as the Platt Amendment, imposed on the new government by the U.S. Senate.

*Page 103

Federico Laredo Brú. One of a parade of puppet presidents under the thumb of Batista's rule. Brú's administration extended from 1936 to 1940.